PRAISE FOR VANESSA'S VALENTINE

Four-time award-winning author

"AMAZING! A fantastic, well written read. An intense storyline that holds your attention as you get caught up in the fierce twists and hot chemistry. Plenty of excitement and emotionally heart-felt. A thrilling must read."

— BOOKBUB REVIEWER ON VANESSA'S VALENTINE

I0456888

VANESSA'S VALENTINE

A NOVELLA

CB SAMET

Romancing the Spirit

A ROMANCING THE
SPIRIT NOVELLA

VANESSA'S VALENTINE

CB SAMET

Cover Art: Get Covers

Print ISBN: 978-1-950942-12-1

CHAPTER 1

*V*anessa stepped out into the cool February night, carrying her medical bag in one hand and a dozen roses in the other. The balance was precarious as she tried to hug the heavy, rose-laden vase close to her body, while at the same time not get impaled by the gazillion tiny thorns along the stems of the beautiful flowers.

Where in her minuscule house was she going to put this ostentatious, gargantuan bouquet?

She slipped the straps of her medical bag up high on her forearm and freed one hand in order to open the door of her electric blue Ford Fiesta. She carefully positioned the vase in the passenger seat, cushioning it with her medical bag so it wouldn't fall forward.

After closing the door, she walked around the front of the car and sank into the driver's seat. Outside, the sun had nearly set, and the clinic parking lot sat vacant. A single floodlight lit the small brick building.

Just as she pushed the START button on her car, the

door behind her opened. The car jolted as someone landed in the back seat—before slamming the door shut behind them.

"Drive!" a male voice commanded.

Jumping in her seat, Vanessa looked into the rearview mirror to find a bearded man in a sweatsuit half-sitting, half-slouching in the back seat.

"Get out of my car!" she screamed, heart rate spiking with fear.

A loud crack coincided with the shattering of her back window.

She ducked lower in her seat. "Is someone *shooting* at you?"

"Drive!" the intruder barked again.

This time, Vanessa slammed her car into drive and peeled out of the parking lot. She sped north on the highway, the engine of her small car whining in protest.

She glanced in the rearview mirror to see a pickup truck tailing them. Gripping the wheel tightly as adrenaline surged through her body, she embraced her flight mode.

"What the hell is going on?" she demanded.

"Those men work for Julio Oquiñena. He's a Mexican drug dealer."

"And *you* are?"

"My name is Seth Dellosa. I'm an undercover DEA agent." Seth winced as she swerved to avoid a pothole.

"I'm supposed to believe you?"

"I'm hoping the truth will motivate you to help me."

"If they're shooting at you, I'd guess you're not so

undercover anymore." Her voice was harsh with the strain of keeping her composure during the car chase.

Seth snorted. "Yeah, I *was* undercover."

"Are you armed?"

"No."

Vanessa couldn't decide if this stranger being unarmed gave her more comfort or less. She glanced in the rearview mirror. "They're still following us."

"Can you lose them?"

Her heart thumped wildly against her rib cage as she navigated the back roads at a terrifying velocity. Fortunately, part of her family medicine practice involved making house calls, so she knew these roads as well as she knew every organ in the human body.

When she looked down at Seth through the rearview mirror, she noticed streaks of blood on her tan, partial leather seat.

:You're injured."

"Very astute of you, Dr. Watson."

A chill spread through Vanessa—one that competed with the heat from the fear coursing through her. "How do you know who I am?"

She'd just walked out of her own clinic and this *was* small town Texas—yet something about him knowing her name and identity spooked her. Had he been waiting in the parking lot for her, specifically? For Dr. Vanessa Watson?

"Right now, that's not important," the DEA agent insisted. "What's important is that you get us away from Julio's men."

She slammed on the brakes and made a sharp right

turn onto a narrow road. The roses and vase tumbled onto the passenger side floor of the car.

In the backseat, Seth groaned.

She navigated the road with its many potholes expertly. She could tell by the erratic headlights behind her that the pickup truck was hitting most of those potholes with the ferocity of a game of Whack-a-Mole. Since their pursuers couldn't maintain their high speeds *and* navigate the numerous road hazards, the distance between the two vehicles started to lengthen.

Fifty feet before the road morphed into a wider, two-lane highway, she cut off her headlights. She made a sharp turn left and accelerated.

After several twists and turns on the dark road, she clicked on her headlights again. She couldn't continue to drive in the dark and risk hitting a deer or a bobcat. Still, she no longer saw headlights behind them.

Taking slow, steady breaths, she tried to ease her body out of flight mode. She'd never been shot at before, and her tight grip had likely made imprints on her steering wheel. She'd never been in a high-speed car chase before, either—and she'd certainly never had a man claiming to be a DEA agent bleeding in the backseat of her car.

Vanessa thought about where she was on these rural Texas back roads and began calculating their proximity to the nearest hospital—which wasn't quite so near. "I'll take you to Corpus Christi Hospital."

"No," Seth barked.

"I don't know the extent of your injuries," Vanessa shot back, "but at first glance it looks like you're bleeding, pale, and dehydrated. You need a hospital."

"I came to you for help precisely because it's not *safe* for me to go to a hospital. Julio would be able to find me in a hospital."

Vanessa clenched her jaw. It wasn't safe for her to do anything *other* than take him to a hospital. If she delivered this injured agent to a qualified medical facility, he could at least receive police protection—if he truly was the DEA agent he claimed to be.

Seth's words echoed in her mind. *I came to you for help.* The tone of his voice and the sincerity of that statement had been partially pleading.

No, no, no.

Helping this man outside of a controlled medical environment was *not* a good idea.

Vanessa gripped the wheel tighter to steel her resolve. "Look—I'm really not into getting shot at, or whatever other maiming those men have in mind. If they did that to *you*, I'm sure they'll have no compunction about killing *me*. We're going to a hospital."

Seth didn't reply.

She turned and looked in the backseat, where the bleeding DEA agent lay. He was unconscious, but his chest rose and fell, and she could see the soft pulsation of his carotid artery.

Vanessa swore. She couldn't let him die in the backseat of her car on the way to the hospital. She needed to give him emergency medical care right now.

SETH'S LEG throbbed as the car came to a stop with the sound of crunching gravel. The door opened, and Vanessa Watson tugged him upright. Her long red hair fell in loose ringlets over her shoulders. So close to her, he noticed a small cluster of freckles trailing across her nose.

"Looks like a gunshot wound to your leg. Do you have any other major injuries?"

"Where are we?" Seth asked.

"*La casa del doctora*," Rico told him. "She didn't take you to *el hospital*. I told you—you can trust her."

"Um. Safehouse," Vanessa replied.

"*Ella vive sola?*" Seth asked Rico. Vanessa wouldn't be able to hear Rico Valez's response. Rico was a ghost—and very few people could hear or see ghosts.

"*Sí*," Rico replied.

Vanessa helped Seth to his feet. "You should know my Spanish is a work in progress … if you're going to insist on going back and forth between English and Spanish."

"*Es este lugar seguro?*" Seth asked Rico.

"*Sí. Solamente un perro.*"

"Great. You're delirious." Vanessa sighed.

Seth's former partner, Rico, hovered beside him—a translucent shadow of his former self. Rico followed as the doctor assisted Seth, moving him toward her house and helping him keep most of his weight on his right—uninjured—leg. With every excruciating step, Seth felt like someone was driving a knife into his thigh.

Vanessa's house was a small, ancient-looking wood cabin with a tiny, rickety porch. In the dim evening light, Seth could make out trees along the boundary of what appeared to be about ten acres or so of ungrazed pastureland. Seth eyed the black Labrador standing on the porch, greeting them with a robustly wagging tail.

"Don't worry about Crick, he's friendly," Vanessa promised.

Seth struggled up the steps, taking them one at a time while simultaneously trying not to crush Vanessa with his weight, or pass out from the pain. Fresh, hot blood oozed from his leg as a cold sweat trickled down his neck.

As if sensing his escalating duress, Vanessa situated herself closer to support him. Seth's nostrils flared as they filled with the scent of her—a combination of roses and honey laced with vanilla. He recalled the roses she'd carried out from her clinic and put in her car. Immediately following that moment, he'd made the decision to climb into her vehicle, dragging her into the danger in his life.

Vanessa managed to unlock the front door while still supporting him. As they entered, she flicked on the light switch. The couch caught his eye, enticing him to lie down and close his eyes.

"Oh no, you don't." She steered him toward her kitchen.

"The kitchen?"

"Oh, we're back to English now?" She helped him onto the counter, where she made Seth lay flat and stretch out his leg.

The hard, uncomfortable surface was the least part of his discomfort. She placed a pillow from the sofa under his head. He felt consciousness slipping away from him.

Then, he felt her gloved hands on him—cutting clothes

and inspecting his injuries. She spoke as she worked, explaining her every move in a soothing voice.

Seth's eyes grew heavy until they closed altogether.

Vanessa worked quickly, flashing back to her year of emergency medicine training. She'd left that career path behind her, but with Seth's injuries before her, she was instantly reminded of the intense pressure and rush of working under a ticking clock on a trauma patient.

She opened her physician bag and lined up her equipment: forceps, bandages, lidocaine and syringe, disinfectant, and suture thread with needle. She cut off Seth's sweatshirt and placed a wristband and electrodes on his exposed skin. The electrodes transmitted wirelessly to the wristband, displaying his electrocardiogram rhythm. The wristband tracked his heart rate and oxygen levels. So far, his vital signs didn't indicate hemorrhagic shock.

With the man's pants now converted to shorts, she applied a pressure dressing to his leg. She'd have to come back to that wound, which had dark venous blood emerging from it—not the bright, brisk arterial blood.

With a handheld ultrasound, she checked his vital organs for damage. There were no collapsed lungs, no blood around his heart, and no hemorrhage in his abdomen. When she finished her assessment, Vanessa inventoried his injuries: a gunshot wound to the leg, which appeared to be through and through the muscle, plus a laceration to his right forearm needing stitches, and a host of superficial bruising. Seth had taken a beating before or after taking the bullet.

8

She looked at the sleeping stranger. His beard extended longer than the dark, sweaty hair plastered to his head. She'd cut off his shirt and most of his sweatpants. His toned body boasted defined musculature, but wasn't bulky. He had no track marks and good dentition, so while it remained to be seen whether he was friend or foe, he wasn't a junkie. That would make him easier to sedate. Considering the work she still needed to do—not to mention the pain it would induce—Vanessa didn't want a startled, disoriented patient waking and lashing out at her.

She started an IV and hung a bag of saline. Then, she roused Seth and helped him take oral narcotics to keep him comfortable. When he lay back once again, he closed his eyes. She watched his vital signs as she disinfected, anesthetized tissue, sutured, and bandaged.

Crick, who'd been quietly lying on his rug watching her, whined.

"Right, food. Sorry, boy." Vanessa broke away from doctoring to feed the hungry Lab.

After she took care of Crick, Vanessa removed Seth's cowboy boots. She took his wallet from his back pocket, opened it, and stared at the driver's license within.

"Jorge Hernandez, huh?"

She looked again at the dozing, half-naked man on her kitchen counter. Despite the paleness of his skin from the blood loss, Seth had a clearly dark complexion—suggesting potentially Hispanic origins. His Spanish sounded beautifully melodic, too—yet his English had been crisp, without a Spanish accent.

Vanessa needed to get Seth—or Jorge, or whoever this

man was—off her countertop. She had a bed or a couch to offer, but the couch was too short for him.

With the liter of fluid almost out, she removed his IV. She hadn't given Seth a comatose level of narcotics, so he should be able to help her move himself.

Here goes nothing.

Vanessa slid an arm underneath him and began to pull the big man upright. "Seth, I need you to wake up and help me move you."

When he stirred and sat up, she helped him swing his legs off the edge of the countertop. Because he didn't grimace, she suspected the combination of local anesthetic and systemic narcotics had sufficiently blunted the pain of his gunshot wound. Fortunately, the bullet hadn't lodged in his leg, so she'd only had to patch him up and not dig around for a foreign object.

"Rico, donde estoy?"

"Oh, I know that one. You want to know where you are. You're at my house. I don't know who Rico is, though. I'm Dr. Watson."

Seth's green eyes focused on her. He reached out his hands and cupped her face. "You are so beautiful."

She gave a nervous chuckle as she dodged his gaze. She positioned herself beside him to help Seth down off the counter.

"That's the drugs talking. I may have been a little generous with the meds as a precaution, for my own safety. You know, I once had a patient tell me he'd give me his gizzard while he was under the influence of benzodiazepines and narcotics. Being a city girl, I had to look up what the heck a gizzard was."

Seth smiled at her, maintaining his intense gaze. "Your hair is amazing. Like a rippling sunset."

"Well, it's winter. You should see this red mane in the Texas heat and humidity. I look like an alpaca. They really should put a warning label on this state for people with long hair thinking of moving here."

He chuckled and seemed unfazed about continuing to stare at Vanessa as if she was a movie star.

"Down you go. Watch the weight on your left leg. You're all patched up, but don't strain anything. I hope your tetanus shot is up to date." She kept those in her office, not at her home.

Vanessa helped Seth through her living room and into her bedroom. When she tried to ease him onto her bed, his weight was too much for her and she was pulled down with him. She drew up her leg, trying not to bump his wound but ended up just straddling him on the bed.

His hands slid along her waist. Her breath hitched at the smooth sensuality of his touch. His calloused palms felt both tantalizing and tender.

"Vanessa." He pulled her closer and pressed his lips to her neck.

The feel of his bare chest, hard body, and hot breath sent heated desire through Vanessa's body.

Impossible.

Logical thought prevailed over hormones as she pushed herself up and off of him. For heaven's sake—she didn't even know this man!

But Seth smiled knowingly, as though aware she'd pushed away despite the sparks flying between them. Seeing that he knew the effect he'd had on her, even if only for a moment, hardened Vanessa's resolve. She began to move further away, but hesitated when Seth's dark green eyes looked at her with something like adoration. Then, she saw his constricted pupils, reminding her that he was buzzing under the influence of the narcotics she'd given him.

"You felt amazing," Seth said in a husky rasp.

"Yes, well—you're already expressing yourself *without* words." She avoided looking at the part of him that seemed to want her the most. Getting shot and drugged didn't seem to impact his ability to become noticeably aroused.

"Thank you for helping me."

Vanessa looked down at the floor and rubbed the sole of her shoe along a zigzag design on the gray carpet. "Get some rest."

"What about you?"

"I'll be in the other room if you need anything."

He nodded. "I'm sorry for the trouble."

Vanessa wanted desperately to ask him how bad the trouble was. What danger had she exposed herself to in helping this handsome stranger? But she'd save those questions for when they were both better rested.

"Vanessa?"

"Yes."

"What day is it?"

"February fourteenth. Valentine's Day." Vanessa pulled the door to her bedroom shut as she left.

CHAPTER 2

*V*anessa woke to Crick's excited woofs. When he exited through the doggy flap in the front door, she groaned. The morning sun streamed through her blinds, but it was still way too early for company. By the time she'd cleaned all the blood and medical utensils in her kitchen and wound down from a car chase and a trauma, it had been two in the morning.

A knock at the door. "Vanessa?"

Ugh. How could Gregg possibly be up and perky this early?

She threw off the afghan and stood to answer the door.

"Wait." Seth's quiet word of caution halted her. He emerged from down the hall, holding a gun.

"You found my *gun?*" Vanessa whispered harshly.

"You shouldn't put a stranger in the same room as your firearm."

Vanessa put her hands on her hips as her blood began

to boil. "You would've had to dig through my underwear drawer to find it!"

Her father had bought her the gun when he'd learned she planned to move to a remote house in rural Texas and live alone. So far, the only thing she'd shot at had been a rattlesnake Crick had found.

Seth shrugged.

"Vanessa, are you in there?"

"Let me get the door," Seth said.

"No. You go back into hiding. I'll take care of Gregg."

"Gregg?"

"Shoo."

Vanessa smoothed her hair back and opened the door. She stepped out onto the porch and closed the door behind her. "Good morning, Gregg."

Gregg, the local county sheriff, stood on Vanessa's porch with his felt campaign hat in his hand. He gave Vanessa a beaming smile—all white teeth and rosy cheeks framed by an impeccable blond crew cut. He wore the tan uniform of his department, neatly pleated.

"Did you like the flowers?" he asked.

Vanessa's eyes cut to her car—where she'd left the roses she'd been bringing home scattered all over the passenger footwell. She'd completely forgotten about them, what with a man shot and bleeding in her backseat. She might have remembered the roses earlier—if she hadn't been fantasizing about Seth's hands all over her.

She cleared her throat. "They were—*are*—beautiful."

"I called this morning, but you didn't answer. I'm sorry to disrupt your morning."

Phone.

14

Vanessa hadn't placed it on the charger because the charger was in the same room as the seductive DEA agent, and she knew better than to go back in there. The battery was probably dead.

"Work ran late. I slept in."

"I'd like a second date." Gregg's meek tone held a slight inflection of a question. "This Friday is the town's Valentine dance."

"Work has been a little backed up. I'm not sure when a good time will be."

When Gregg didn't conceal his disappointment, Vanessa winced. He was an incredibly nice guy—polite, gracious, and chivalrous to the point he'd probably throw his coat down should a puddle threaten to accost a lady's shoes. He had an innocent chasteness that had him blushing with anything so much as handholding.

Vanessa appreciated all of those traits, but she couldn't thrive in a relationship without passion and humor. She'd found throughout medical school and residency that she absolutely *needed* humor in her life to balance the hardships and heartbreak of practicing medicine. On their one date so far, Gregg had demonstrated that he either didn't have a sense of humor, or he didn't know how to relate to hers.

"I'll check back with you." Gregg backed his way toward his police cruiser.

"Absolutely—and I'll charge my phone so I can answer your call next time."

It would be far better for the Sheriff to call her next time, rather than arrive unannounced on her doorstep and discover the stranger she was harboring—the stranger who'd led someone to shoot out her rear window and who'd bled all over her car.

Her stomach lurched. As Gregg left the porch, he started to walk past her car, this time with the rear window in full view.

She hurried down the steps to escort him to his cruiser, hoping to distract him. "I *do* appreciate the roses." She hooked an arm through his to keep his bright eyes focused on her rather than the obvious damage to her car.

"I hate you had to work late on Valentine's Day," Gregg sighed.

"I worked very late."

Thanks to an impromptu trauma victim.

That being said, she also had *no* intention of spending a second date with anyone at a Valentine's event—that suggested way too much commitment, way too soon.

He reached his police cruiser—every surface and speck of chrome of which gleamed spotlessly in the Texas sunshine. It was a stark contrast to her own messy car. "You should get some rest today."

"No rest for the weary. I've got house calls to make."

Gregg climbed inside his car and set his sheriff's hat on the passenger seat. "I'll see you around."

The way her luck was spiraling on a downward trajectory, he was probably right.

After closing his door, she watched the Sheriff loop around and drive down her driveway. He gave one last wave out the driver's side window as he left.

When the cruiser was out of sight, Vanessa went to her own car and retrieved the roses, piling them haphazardly in her arms and dragging the empty vase out after them. When she reached her porch, laden with the flowers, Seth opened the door for her. She marched straight past him and dumped the flowers on the counter.

"Was that your boyfriend?"

"That's none of your business."

"Are the flowers from him?"

"They are." She filled the vase with water and began jabbing the stems back into the vase.

"They don't seem to make you happy." He crossed his arms. She could feel him watching her—and that fueled her fuming temper.

"The florist should've removed the thorns. Rose thorns can carry disease, you know." She sucked on a finger where a thorn had stabbed her.

Seth limped into the kitchen and stood near Vanessa. She dabbed a paper towel on her cuts without looking at Seth. What was this infuriating magnetism she felt around him? She didn't even like beards. Did she?

He took her hand in his. "I don't think you're angry at the roses."

"Of course, I am. They carry sporotrichosis. Nasty infection." She added the last words a bit breathlessly at his touch.

Seth took the antiseptic, which still sat on her counter from treating his own injuries the previous night, and dabbed some on her cuts with cotton swabs. "You're angry at me—and that's okay. Completely justified. I've inconvenienced you and put you in danger. We can talk about all of that, and I'll be out of your way as soon as I'm well enough."

Vanessa took her hand back from his—slowly, almost reluctantly. "Thanks. I need to get ready for work."

SETH WATCHED Vanessa stomp toward her bedroom. He'd set the gun down on the kitchen table after the Sheriff had left, but she'd never attempted to retrieve it. As angry as this woman was at him—and justifiably so—she clearly didn't fear him. If she had, she'd have regained possession of her weapon.

Seth hadn't actually been the one to discover the doctor's gun. Rico had told him where it was hidden—ghosts had a sixth sense about some things. When Seth had heard a car approaching Vanessa's home, he'd had to weigh the risk of pissing Vanessa off—by going through her lingerie drawer to retrieve the gun—against the benefits of being prepared for a possible assault.

"You didn't mention she was dating the sheriff," Seth told Rico.

"*No lo sé.*" Rico's squat apparition appeared and shrugged.

"That complicates things."

"*Por qué?*"

"Because I need to lie low until I'm healed, or until I can talk with my boss about bringing down Julio. I can't have Barney Fife snooping around. Julio's got dozens of dirty cops who report to him. If this cop-boyfriend—Gregg—finds me and that knowledge gets into the wrong hands..." Seth's voice trailed as he busied himself pulling out each rose and shearing off the thorns with a kitchen knife before carefully arranging the flowers back into the vase.

"You didn't apologize for groping Vanessa last night," Rico said.

Seth glanced irritably in the ghost's direction. "If I had, she'd probably have detected insincerity in my voice. I need to build trust. It's probably best if we pretend it didn't happen."

"You're not sorry?"

"It was completely inappropriate, and I was on drugs, but I can't claim to regret touching her."

While Vanessa showered, Seth located the dog food and fed Crick. Seth might be injured, but he wasn't an invalid and he refused to be useless. He then went out to Vanessa's car and cleaned up the blood and shattered glass. Her location was rural enough that he felt confident he wouldn't be seen from the driveway.

He owed her a new rear window for her car. He owed her his life.

Back inside, he washed his hands and set to work making breakfast. He sizzled bacon, fried eggs, and toasted bread. He turned on the coffee maker and set it brewing.

When Vanessa emerged, she looked refreshed and composed. Her red hair had been tamed into loose waves, while light makeup adorned her porcelain skin. In a frenzy of activity, she packed her doctor's bag—full of impressively high-tech tools—and slung it over her shoulder.

"Cream, or sugar, or both?" Seth asked.

She turned toward him. "Cream."

He added half-and-half and handed her coffee in a thermal mug. With unconcealed surprise, Vanessa took the cup from him slowly—as if it might shatter at any moment. As she sipped the coffee, she scanned the prepared breakfast food.

"Peace offering," Seth explained.

"Thanks, but, uh... I... I have to go—I don't want to be late for my house call." Her cheeks deepened from a flushed pink to crimson red.

His brow furrowed. Had making her breakfast upset her? Quickly, he threw the toast, bacon, egg, and slice of cheese together into a sandwich. After wrapping it in tinfoil, he handed it to her.

"Thank you," she said. "You need to get that leg elevated and stop putting so much weight on it. Also, there's ibuprofen and acetaminophen in the cabinet. You should alternate taking them every six hours."

Seth pressed his hands together. "Vanessa, can I talk you into calling in sick today? I'm worried about your safety if those men recognize your car around town."

"I have patients waiting to be seen. I have to make these house calls."

"Then I'll go with you."

"Absolutely not."

As if on command, his leg began throbbing in protest at the idea of cramming into that tiny car. He leaned heavily on the counter to take weight off his injury. "Okay —but then, will you at least not go anywhere near your office? Julio's men arrived after you exited the building, but they might still return looking for clues."

Vanessa cocked her head to one side, considering his request. "I can do that."

"Okay. Good. And can you take your gun with you?"

"I don't have a license to carry a concealed weapon."

"Even if a DEA agent tells you to?"

She arched an eyebrow and quirked her lips. "You claim you're a DEA agent—but your wallet says you're Jorge Hernandez."

"My alias."

"So you tell me."

"You win. I have no proof of who I am, but please be safe."

When Vanessa looked at him—with her red hair in large, silky curls, her coffee in one hand and the sandwich in the other—he felt an instant connection between them. He'd felt the same connection when he'd wrapped his arms around her last night, but he'd attributed those feelings to the drugs. Now, he could tell the chemistry between them was unmistakably tangible.

Did she feel it too? Or were those wide, blue eyes of hers wishing he was already out of her home? Out of her life?

Seth wanted to close the distance between them and gauge her reaction, but the idea seemed preposterous. They'd only just met, and his intrusion into her home posed a threat to her life.

The redhead turned and left. "Rest that leg," she called out over her shoulder as the door closed behind her.

. . .

VANESSA WAS SURPRISED to discover that Seth had cleaned her car, and aside from the absence of a rear window and the bullet hole in the passenger side headrest, her vehicle showed no other evidence of the previous night's chaos.

Seth had cleaned her car, right before he'd made her breakfast. Breakfast! When was the last time a man had cooked Vanessa breakfast? Never.

It had seemed like such a sweet and intimate gesture that she hadn't known how to respond to it. At first, she hadn't wanted to accept the gesture, because she'd only ever imagined somebody making breakfast for her—in the intimacy of her own home—within the context of a deep relationship. Then there'd been the confounding issue that Seth had been shirtless as he'd presented coffee and breakfast to her. Again, this seemed like it should only occur after a night of passionate intimacy. But Vanessa had cut his shirt off, so what else could he be except shirtless?

Treating Seth as a patient had been intimate, but dispassionate—right up until he'd placed his hands on her and his body responded visibly to their proximity.

As she drove away, she sank her teeth into the sandwich Seth had packaged for her. She was famished after skipping dinner to tend to him last night.

A man had cooked her breakfast. Correction: A shirtless man with playful green eyes had cooked her breakfast. How could Vanessa turn this into a platonic gesture in her mind, so that she could properly process it?

TWENTY MINUTES LATER, Vanessa pulled into Mrs. Johnson's driveway. The home of her first patient was secluded, set on a few acres of land covered with wiry scutch grass, in desperate need of mowing. Mrs. Johnson was an aged diabetic who couldn't drive due to a combination of poor vision and peripheral neuropathy.

"Dr. Watson, I presume?" Mrs. Johnson asked with a smile playing on her lips. She rose from the rocking chair where she'd been sitting on her porch. "I'd know that red hair a half-mile away."

"How are you, Mrs. Johnson?" Vanessa climbed the steps and patted the woman's hand.

Mrs. Johnson sat back down in her rocking chair. She'd told Vanessa during her very first visit that she'd prefer her check-up to take place on her porch, as it had the most relaxing view. Since then, Vanessa had obliged.

"Well, another sunrise has blessed these old bones. What about you? Did you have a pleasant Valentine's Day?"

Well, I was up half the night treating a trauma victim, who's now a guest in my house, armed with my revolver.

"I stayed in," Vanessa replied, as she squirted hand sanitizer into her palms and rubbed her hands together. She took out her blood pressure cuff and wrapped it around her patient's arm.

"Young thing like you ought to have been having a nice, romantic dinner."

"I had to work late." She signed into her electronic tablet, selected Mrs. Johnson from her patient list, and opened her chart. "But I did get flowers."

CB SAMET

"How lovely."

Vanessa glanced at the tiny scratches on her hand, carved by the sharp thorns of the roses. The nicest part about the flowers was Seth holding her hand and gently dabbing disinfecting solution on her cuts.

For all she knew, the man could right now be robbing her blind—not that she had much worth stealing, except her medical gadgets—which were all with her. But for some reason, she doubted he was robbing her. Besides, where could he go with what meager things he could have stolen? He had no vehicle, no money, and there was no landline at her place to call anyone.

Vanessa performed a physical exam on Mrs. Johnson before drawing her blood. The drops went directly into a small, pocket-sized analyzer.

"I made you a blackberry pie."

"I appreciate that, Mrs. Johnson—but we talked about a low-carb diet."

"I made *you* a pie—not me—and I'm doing the intermittent fasting you suggested. I do feel like I've got more energy."

"Wonderful. Well, your vital signs are good, as are your electrolytes. I'll have to send off the rest of the blood sample for your kidney function and cholesterol panel."

"You'll let me know what those show?"

"I certainly will."

"Well, c'mon inside and get your pie."

JULIO OQUIÑENA CLIPPED the end of his cigar and lit it. He'd been told he was too young to have such an affinity for delectable cigars, but he considered himself an old soul. The Royal Jamaica cigar soothed his hot-headed tendencies and temper, as it bought him time to reflect rather than react. His ability to maintain rational, logical thought had enabled him to rise in the ranks in *Las Arañas*.

Julio's second in command, Val, stood off to one corner watching him—probably fantasizing about his next meal while Pancho sweated profusely in front of him.

"So, to summarize—" Julio took a long, leisurely drag on the cigar, "—Rico Valez and Jorge Hernandez were working undercover against me. We discovered Rico, who ratted on Jorge—with some forceful convincing—but somehow Jorge got away. His escape means he could be taking all of his knowledge about our organization to whichever agency he works for."

"Rico said DEA," Pancho offered, wringing his hands together, "and he also said Jorge's real name was Seth, but he didn't know his last name."

"So, now I can expect a visit from the DEA?"

Pancho's throat bobbed in a swallow. "I shot him."

"Dead or alive?"

Val crossed his arms, looking irritated at Pancho's nervous behavior. "I checked all the hospitals. No one fitting Jorge's description has shown up. And there are no news reports about deaths near the border."

"So, he's either holed up somewhere—or dead and

undiscovered. Until I see a body, let's assume he's not dead."

"I'll find him," Pancho said.

"Oh, I think you've done enough." Julio had many reasons to get involved personally in the apprehension of Jorge—no, *Seth*. The information the traitor knew about Julio's organization simply couldn't be allowed to fall into the hands of the DEA.

Also, Julio needed to get his hands dirty every once in a while—if only to demonstrate to his followers that he was still a ruthless force to revere. Lastly, this had now become personal. Julio had shared secrets with—and confided in—Jorge, believing he was a valuable asset to *Las Arañas*. They'd spent many tranquil nights together talking and plotting over a fine blue agave tequila.

"Val and I will go after Jorge Hernandez."

"*Tu brazo*," Julio added.

Pancho took a shaky breath before extending his forearm. He rolled up the sleeve of his shirt to reveal a circular scar of pale, puckered skin. He steeled himself, gripping the bicep of the exposed arm with his other hand.

Early in his career, Julio learned that loyalty proved far more effectively secured when his men felt they owed him something. Rather than waste loyalty by killing someone who'd failed him, he secured loyalty by sparing their lives. Yet, only so many mistakes could be tolerated. Julio enjoyed baseball, so he'd adopted the 'three-strikes-and-you're-out' philosophy.

Julio took one last drag on his cigar before burying the glowing red tip in Pancho's arm, directly beside the other round scar. To his credit, although Pancho turned three shades of purple before going white, he didn't cry out. When Julio pulled the stubbed-out cigar from Pancho's scalded flesh, Pancho collapsed into a nearby chair.

Julio gave him a cold, hard stare. "You have one strike left."

CHAPTER 3

Seth invaded Vanessa's personal space. He felt guilty looking through her drawers and cabinets, but he didn't know his way around her house. Eventually, he found what he needed—a razor, shaving cream, a clean towel, plastic wrap, her largest t-shirt, and her baggiest sweatpants.

He wrapped the dressed wounds on his leg and arm with plastic wrap so he could shower. After then shaving and dressing in her borrowed clothes, he cleaned up the mess he'd created in her bathroom.

"What's a doctor doing in such a tiny home? Two bedrooms, one and a half bathrooms? I thought doctors had five-thousand square-foot homes with a Jacuzzi and a sauna." Seth sat down in Vanessa's home office and opened her laptop.

"They're not all rich," Rico said, materializing into the room.

Seth glanced at his partner—former partner. Damn. He felt bad his partner had been killed. If Julio's men hadn't killed Rico, his friend wouldn't have turned into a ghost, giving him the power to find and warn Seth that Julio's men were coming for him next. Rico's death was the only reason Seth was still alive. Seth didn't begrudge Rico for outing him. He'd seen enough of Julio's enemies horrifically tortured to know that keeping secrets from that sadistic bastard was practically impossible.

Seth's gaze fell upon a photo on Vanessa's desk. In a decorative yellow frame, she was hugging her friendly black Lab.

Seth picked up the picture. "What she doesn't have in money, she makes up for in beauty. Be still, my heart," he added in wistful playfulness.

He set down the photo when the computer had powered up. "I wasn't implying there's anything wrong with a modest home," he told Rico. "Maybe it's my own stereotype about doctors—or maybe she's got bad debt."

"No bad debt, *amigo*. She took a job in rural Texas as part of a medical student loan forgiveness program. She's wed to this place for the next four years."

Seth was always amazed by what information ghosts were capable of gleaning from people. It seemed random —and most of the time, when he asked a specific question, ghosts were generally clueless. However, enough of them had drifted in and out of his life over the years, sharing helpful details, that he'd come to value them and nurture his relationship with them when they agreed to linger.

Vanessa's computer screen opened with a prompt
USERNAME: Watson09
PASSWORD: _____
"I don't suppose you know her computer password?"

"No," Rico said.

"What's '09 stand for?"

"*No lo sé.*"

Once again invading her privacy, Seth looked through Vanessa's drawers and papers.

"I can tell you her birthdate and social," Rico offered.

"It wouldn't be that simple." Seth leaned back and gazed around the room.

Pictures adorned one wall—a series of black and white photos of Vanessa and her dog. Another wall held a bookcase filled with a haphazard collection of medical texts, cookbooks, and J.D. Robb thriller novels.

Seth rotated Vanessa's desk chair a full three-hundred-sixty degrees. When he came back to her desk, he saw a stack of bills and the photo he'd picked up moments earlier—a full-color selfie of her and the dog. The personalized frame said, "Watson and Crick."

"I bet her password has her dog's name in it." Seth noticed her old desk had been designed for a desktop computer and had a built-in sliding keyboard tray. He rolled the tray towards him.

"Jackpot," Rico said.

The keyboard tray didn't hold a keyboard, but it did have two-dozen sticky notes with various user-names and passwords.

Rico whistled. "Only fifty to choose from."

"This one." Taking a guess, Seth entered the password "Crick70", and Vanessa's desktop icons appeared.

Her computer backdrop showed a photo of Crick running on a beach. Seth thought about the sheriff and the roses he'd brought her. Vanessa must not yet be in a serious relationship with Gregg, since Seth saw no photos of them together as a couple either in her house or on her computer screen backdrop.

Seth opened a web browser and logged into his email. He typed a message to his superior—Jody Green. Seth needed Jody to know he was alive, but his cover had been blown. He would come into the DEA offices in San Antonio when he felt it was safe to do so. Before sending the email, he routed it through a dummy IP address, so it couldn't be traced to Vanessa's house.

Next, Seth did a search on Dr. Vanessa Watson.

Rico crossed his translucent, ghostly arms. "You're cyber-stalking the woman who saved your life?"

"I'm investigating." Seth scanned through what the search engine revealed.

"I told you she's on the level."

"Yes—and you were right to send me to her. Now that I'm coherent and not exhausted from trauma and blood loss, I need to make sure it's safe to stay here for a few days."

"Safe for you? Or her?"

"Mostly her. Well, her name is associated with the clinic—I saw the sign when I got into her car, but I doubt *Las Arañas* saw her license plate from that distance in the dark. And I doubt they got a good look at Vanessa herself, although that red hair would be memorable if they saw it."

"Besides, what kind of physician drives such an... *economical* car?"

"Well, hopefully, *Las Arañas* will be that stereotypical. Even if they make all the wrong assumptions, they may still track down all the employees of the clinic—talk to them, coerce them, or whatever it takes to uncover the information they want."

"Or they could simply check the local auto shops to see who's replacing a rear window. They know they hit the car."

Seth pulled up information about Dr. Watson's clinic. "It looks like only Vanessa and an assistant work at the clinic. Hours are Monday, Tuesdays, and Thursdays. Wednesdays are by appointment only. I'm guessing Wednesdays are her days for house calls, since it's Wednesday today—and that's what she's off doing."

Rico stared at the screen over Seth's shoulder. "Not bad hours."

"Maybe she does house calls Friday, too."

Rico shook his head. "House calls. That's old school, *hombre*."

"Except she's high tech. Did you see the equipment she loaded in her doctor bag?" Seth's leg began to ache, so he elevated it on her desk.

"I saw what she did for you ... *to* you. Ultrasounds and monitors. I didn't understand half of it."

Seth stared at the photo of Vanessa and Crick as he ran a hand through his hair. "I put an innocent woman's life in danger by getting in her car, Rico."

"You'd be dead right now if you hadn't."

Seth felt torn between the desire to leave Vanessa's home—and take the danger shadowing him away from her—and the desire to stay and protect her from his demons.

"She may not find that a consolation if *Las Arañas* come for her."

Unfortunately, leaving Vanessa might not make her any safer. He couldn't relocate and risk Julio discovering Vanessa, or the aid she'd given Seth. "Keeping her safe may mean staying here until Julio is behind bars."

"And spending time with a beautiful woman is a bonus."

"Yes, it is."

Vanessa was intelligent, good-natured, and attractive. She was also way out of his league. And she had a boyfriend.

VANESSA CALLED her assistant as she drove to her next patient's home.

"Dr. Watson, how's the morning route?"

"Wonderful, Kailee. Any issues?"

"A few medication refills."

Kailee worked from home when Vanessa made house calls. This simultaneously kept the clinic electric bill down, kept Kailee's work hours manageable, and kept Kailee happy because she was able to spend more time at home with her toddler. Patient calls, billing, and scheduling were all manageable with a laptop and mobile phone.

"How does tomorrow look?" Vanessa could pull up her clinic schedule on her tablet, but not while she was driving.

Kailee rattled off the names of four patients in the office and two house calls.

"I hate to do this," —Vanessa *really* hated to do this,

because she needed the money— "but I've got an urgent house call tomorrow." *At my own house.* "Can you reschedule the in-office visits to next week, and I'll see the two house calls?"

"Sure thing. Everything okay?"

"Yes. You can work from home tomorrow, too."

"Okay. Is the urgent house call anyone I know?"

"No. The patient is new to my practice." As new to her practice as his body was to her bedroom sheets.

"I'll process their insurance if you send me the information."

"Okay. Thanks, Kailee." Vanessa hadn't once thought about Seth's insurance status, not while saving his life.

Raw medicine. She'd had such freedom during her residency days. Her job then had simply been to treat and learn. She'd even considered a specialty in emergency medicine because she could treat everyone regardless of their ability to pay. Now, she had company bills to pay and an employee to consider.

"Anything else?" Kailee asked.

"No, thanks a bunch." Vanessa disconnected the call.

The phone-to-car Bluetooth connection retrieved the last audio app she'd been listening to and began playing her Spanish lesson.

"*Tengo hambre.* I am hungry."

Vanessa clicked it off. She couldn't practice Spanish through the distraction of worrying about what awaited her at home. Maybe Seth would be gone—a leaf in the wind. She doubted that. He'd wanted to remain out of sight, and her house probably granted the right amount of remoteness for him.

If he wasn't gone? What then? Vanessa didn't run a rehab facility for trauma patients—and she certainly didn't run a safe-house for DEA agents. That's if he *was* a DEA agent, like he'd claimed. If he wasn't, she certainly didn't run a homeless shelter.

Vanessa thought about Seth's appearance—his long beard and filthy clothes, but healthy skin and good teeth. No, he wasn't homeless.

She checked the clock on her dashboard as she pulled into her next patient's driveway. In a few hours, she'd either find a stranger in her house—one who owed her an explanation—or he'd already be gone.

IN MID AFTERNOON, Julio stood in the parking lot of a small brick building. The sign by the road read: WATSON FAMILY PRACTICE.

He turned to look at Val. "This is where you and Pancho chased Seth to?"

"*Sí.*"

Julio pulled out his phone and looked up the clinic hours. "What time did he get here?"

"6:45 pm."

"The parking lot was empty?"

"Except for the getaway car. We didn't see who else was in the car."

"The clinic hours say *ocho a cinco*, so it was closed. No employees' cars were here. *Ase que*, did he come here to get care because he had a bullet wound? Or did this just happen to be a rendezvous point for whoever picked him up?"

"I don't know. We've made calls trying to track down Seth Anybody in the DEA. Nobody is giving us any information. He's either MIA or not DEA. Rico might also have lied—so if Seth made a scheduled rendezvous with someone here, it might not have been the DEA."

"A friend? A family member?"

"We're looking into that."

"Unless it wasn't a scheduled rendezvous." Julio pulled out a cigar and tapped it against his chin, but he didn't light it. "Jorge—I mean, *Seth*—didn't have his phone, *correcto*? We had it, according to Pancho. It would be hard to schedule a rendezvous *con no teléfono*. So, let's say he happened upon someone in the parking lot *aquí*. Maybe an assistant who happened to be closing up shop?"

"Could be." Val rolled his shoulders.

Julio examined his surroundings again. He stood beside what could be bloodstains on the asphalt. Broken glass—small, square chunks as if from a tempered window—littered the ground nearby. He picked up a single rose petal and pressed the velvety texture between his fingertips.

The clinic was closed today, which seemed suspicious to Julio. He pressed the number on his phone from the clinic website.

A woman answered, "Watson Family Practice."

He infused cheer into his voice. He wouldn't be able to hide his Hispanic accent, but neither did a third of the state of Texas. "Hi, I'm wondering, are you open today?"

"Dr. Watson is doing house calls today, so the clinic is

closed, but I can schedule something for you over the phone."

"You know, I'll have to call back when I have my calendar in front of me. Say, I drove by day before yesterday after five, and the clinic was closed except for one car. Was that you?"

"No. No one from the office would be there after five."

"Okay. Well, I'll give a call back to schedule something with Dr. Watson."

"Great. Talk to you then."

Julio hung up the phone and turned toward Val. "Let's cover all our bases. We need to get a last name for this man and see if any friends or family live close enough to have helped him. While you're doing that, station somebody here at the clinic. If any employees show up, I want to know the plate numbers of their cars, their identities, and if they have a broken window. Check all the hospitals in a fifty-mile radius one more time. Next—*mañana*—canvas all the auto shops in a twenty-mile radius and see if any window repairs turned up."

"You got it."

CHAPTER 4

$\mathcal{V}$anessa pulled into her driveway. The late afternoon sun had warmed mid-February in southern Texas to a pleasant seventy degrees. Having lived in St. Louis during medical school and residency, the weather in Texas had required Vanessa to acclimate to the heat and humidity, but winter here was delightful by comparison.

She rubbed her eyes. The day hadn't been labor intensive—a few patients and a few errands—but staying up late, in addition to the adrenaline depletion from the previous night, had taken its toll.

When Crick wasn't already waiting on the porch for her, in his customary stance with his tail wagging, Vanessa's stomach knotted. Had something happened?

Then, her front door opened, and the Lab came bounding out. Standing in her doorway was—*who is that?*

She took a moment to recognize Seth—who now appeared clean-shaven. He wore a pair of Vanessa's sweatpants, stretched taught over his thighs, and the gray oversized t-shirt she often slept in, which fit him well. When Seth smiled, Vanessa realized she'd never had a man inside this house before. *Her* house. The first house she'd ever owned.

Catching herself staring at Seth, even as she rubbed Crick's ears, she turned with a jerk to unload her car. She pulled out her doctor's bag, purse, and the blackberry pie.

Seth started toward her. "I'll help you."

"Don't you dare! You're supposed to be keeping weight off that leg. You should elevate it." Vanessa tried to use her physician tone, but her voice was still dry from thinking about him wearing her clothes.

"I borrowed some clothes."

She approached the porch. "I noticed." Her eyes inspected Seth from head to toe once again.

He grinned at her again with a slightly smug look. Irritation flushed Vanessa's cheeks at the realization he'd seen her noticing how attractive he looked.

Vanessa narrowed her eyes at him. "I don't even want to think about how many razors you destroyed."

The man had the audacity to chuckle—a pleasant rumble that almost made her smile.

She walked up the steps, passing Seth as she made her way into her house and to the kitchen, where she set down her load. She then walked back outside, down the steps again to fetch the groceries she'd bought.

But something felt off.

Vanessa stopped on the last step and then went back up to press her weight on the middle stair. There was no creaking, familiar instability.

She turned to look at Seth. "Did you fix my steps?"

He had one hand on the porch railing, keeping weight off his injured leg. "It doesn't wobble now, but the entire porch needs replacing."

Vanessa's eyes widened. She turned and walked to her car, where she began unloading groceries from her hatchback. Because it no longer had a rear window, she didn't even have to lift the hatch to grab the bags.

This time, Seth took some of the bags from her and followed her inside, closing the door after Crick followed them in.

"Fixing the board was the least I could do for saving my life."

"You could tell me why you were shot in the first place —and jumped into *my* car last night." Vanessa began putting the groceries away.

Seth leaned on the counter. "Yes, I can do that."

Vanessa stacked part of her purchases. "I bought you a pair of jeans, by the way, plus a pack of t-shirts, and clean underwear." She thrust the clothes at him. "I've no idea if they'll fit." Except she'd touched ninety percent of his body last night, so Vanessa felt confident she'd guessed accurately when choosing sizes for him.

He grinned. "Thanks. Why'd you assume I'd still be here?"

"I *hoped* you'd be smart enough to stay in the care of a medical practitioner, but I assumed nothing." Vanessa waved a white piece of paper in the air and winked at him. "I kept the receipt, just in case you'd left."

When the groceries were put away, she unloaded her medical gadgets and plugged them into their respective chargers on the narrow console table in her living room.

"You've got quite the high-tech operation here." Seth grimaced as he shifted his weight.

"On the couch with you. Elevate your leg."

He obeyed, and she helped him prop pillows beneath his leg.

"Any fresh bleeding?"

"No."

"You've been taking the analgesics?"

"As instructed."

She leaned back with her hands on her hips. His color looked good—fifty shades better than it had last night. The freshly shaved skin was lighter than the rest of his face. She wondered if the men looking for Seth would even recognize him now. She knelt back down to adjust one of the pillows under his leg.

"Yes, my equipment is state-of-the art."

"So are you."

Vanessa turned toward him, placing them at eye level. His face might look different without the beard, but his irises still radiated the same deep green. Shamrock green. Maybe those lucky eyes are what led him to her. Maybe she needed to stop staring at them.

Seth blinked, breaking the intensity of their brief connection. "What I meant is: how many rural physicians could have patched me up the way you did last night?"

"I don't know. Maybe most. Your injuries didn't require major surgery."

"And she's modest, too." Seth chuckled. "*Cuida mi corazón.*"

"Do you always throw in Spanish like that?" She'd understood heart—*corazón*—but not the rest of Seth's phrase. "Last night, I thought it was because you were delirious."

Seth lowered his voice and winked. "I'm communing with the dead."

"Ah, so, still delirious. Anyway," Vanessa continued, "I did a year of residency in emergency room medicine before switching to family medicine—hence, my ability to 'patch you up', as you so eloquently put it."

"Why the switch?"

"After taking care of foul-mouthed, litigious urbanites, I decided I wanted a smaller group of patients—ones I could know and take care of on a personal level. Now, I have that."

"Seems awfully remote."

Vanessa cocked her head to one side, unsure if she'd detected a deeper inference in his words. "Hmm. The under-cover DEA agent is investigating if I'm out here through choice? Or if I'm hiding, or running from something?"

When Vanessa rose to her feet, Seth grasped her hand. The motion flowed—fast, yet gentle.

"Are you hiding, or running?"

What drove Seth's interest in her? Was he reassuring himself she was trustworthy? Vanessa had gone on dates with men who'd asked fewer questions about her than this guy. Was he stalling—so he didn't have to answer her question about his own past?

"Neither," Vanessa answered. "I'm on a government loan repayment program, where each year of rural prac-tice equals a year of medical student loan repayment. I'm afraid I have no tale of woe to impress you with."

"You impressed me the minute you kept your cool while I was bleeding out in your car last night, *and* while *Las Arañas* were shooting at us."

She turned and walked into the kitchen, needing some space from his intensity. "About that. I'm ready for an explanation." She fixed two glasses of water and returned to the couch, handing one to Seth.

"Thanks. Got anything stronger?" He started drinking the water.

"Since my cabinet with the loose handle is now repaired, I'm guessing you already went through my house, so you know the answer to that." She kept her tone firm, but not angry.

Shouldn't she be angry? But he'd fixed things—little things she'd told herself she'd eventually get around to fixing, or paying someone else to do it.

Now, she didn't need to.

"Vanessa…"

"I gave you something stronger last night, and you got frisky." She poked a playful finger into Seth's chest.

He dropped his head. "I shouldn't have done that. You let me into your home and cared for me, and I violated your trust."

"Then there was the gun in my underwear drawer."

"I put it back."

"So, you've been in there *twice* now?" She crossed her arms.

"Sorry." Seth bit his lip with a recalcitrant look that had Vanessa wanting to admit that she'd already forgiven him.

"I also needed to send my boss an email, so I used your laptop," Seth confessed.

She glanced in the direction of the second bedroom, which she'd converted into a home office. "But it's password protected."

His mouth twisted in a 'get real' expression. "The laptop sits on top of a desk, beneath which is a drawer with all of your passwords."

Vanessa let out a defeated huff. "Right. I suppose I'd always imagined a robber stealing my laptop and then trying to access it somewhere else. I never envisioned someone sitting in my office, hacking it right then and there."

"Because your vicious guard dog would keep them away?" Seth grinned.

They both looked at Crick.

"What's the oh-nine stand for?" Seth asked.

"My high school softball number."

"And the seventy?"

"My fast pitch speed—seventy miles per hour."

"Again, I'm sorry," Seth said.

She deflated slightly. "Well, you seem to have pointed out some of my serious security flaws—leaving the clinic alone at night, not being mindful of my surroundings…"

"In all fairness, you were battling some hostile thorns."

"…my lack of a guard dog…"

"But he's adorable."

"…my password hiding spot."

"The keyboard drawer is hardly noticeable."

"My gun drawer!"

"But you store the bullets separately."

Vanessa laughed. "For someone shot and running for their life, you're quite the optimist."

"Still, you do need a security system," Seth warned. "You need an electric gate at the road end of your driveway that also alerts you to company. Since you live alone, you also need a panic alarm to call 9-1-1 immediately."

"What, no panic room? You know this is small town Texas, right?"

"Yes, and just a hop, skip, and a jump away from the border. This area isn't insulated from the war on drugs."

"I'll take your counsel under advisement, agent."

"Of course, with the Sheriff as your boyfriend, you have *some* protection."

"I suppose so." Vanessa wasn't going to dispel Seth's assumption about Gregg. It was none of Seth's business, and it might be useful to let Seth think Gregg might drop by and check on her at any time.

SETH WATCHED VANESSA PREPARE DINNER—RINSING lettuce, chopping tomatoes, peeling cucumbers, and boiling eggs.

He detested lying on the couch idly while she worked, but his leg had started throbbing in the late afternoon—probably precisely because he hadn't spent enough time resting it during the day. He needed to get well—partly to go after Julio, and partly to stop burdening Vanessa.

For several minutes, only chopping and shuffling sounds filled the house.

"I've been undercover for five years," Seth eventually began explaining. "The first year, I built a reputation for keeping my mouth shut, head down, and finishing jobs. During the next few years, I rose in the ranks and learned the smuggling routes. I then partnered with an under-cover agent of the *Policía Federal Ministerial*—Mexican federal government—though you've probably heard of them as Federales. My partner was Rico Valez. We had plans on how we were going to bring down Julio Oquiñena together." Seth rubbed the muscle around his bullet wound. "Someone betrayed Rico. Julio tortured and killed him."

"You lost your partner." She paused her work in the kitchen.

"Two days ago."

"I'm sorry." She resumed tossing the salad.

When the salad was prepared, Seth began to push himself up from the couch. "I can help set the table."

"Stay." She pointed a finger at him.

Pouting, Seth relaxed back onto the couch. Crick padded to him and laid his head in Seth's lap—as if in sympathy to convey that he knew what it felt like to receive that command from Vanessa. Seth rubbed behind the dog's ears. Running his fingers through soft fur felt cathartic, and some of the pain in his leg eased.

Vanessa handed Seth a salad bowl. "Crick, we're eating."

The dog obediently walked to an oval-shaped shag rug by a sliding glass door, which led to the back property. He circled, sniffed, and then curled into a ball.

Vanessa pulled up a chair to sit near the sofa. "Rico was your friend, too?"

"Yeah, we were friends. We talked about one day

basking in the glory of our success when we finally put *Las Arañas* out of business. Rico had a woman he wanted to reveal his true identity to and marry."

"That's tragic."

They ate silently for a few moments.

"How are you going to bring Julio down? You can't go back undercover, right? But since you know Julio's infrastructure and routes, can you turn that over to your superiors?"

Seth shook his head. "It has to be more than a disruption of the workflow. I need a crippling blow to take down Julio and his top men. We need to destroy the pipeline of heroin and amphetamines passing through his organization and into this country."

"'He who can destroy a thing, controls a thing.'"

Seth stared at her. "Did you just quote *Dune*?"

She shrugged. "It's a classic." She grinned. "If only you had a giant worm that could devour Julio for you."

"If only."

Vanessa finished her salad and carried her bowl to the sink. When Seth limped over to join her, she was pouring a glass of wine for herself.

"Do I get one?" he asked.

She slid a plate with a heap of blackberry pie toward him. "Last time…"

"Yes, yes, I got frisky." He remembered how smoothly Vanessa had handled his advances. She'd been flustered, but not angry that a stranger's hands had touched her so intimately.

She twisted, poured a glass for him, and then turned the rest of her body toward him.

Seth eased closer, invading Vanessa's personal space as she rested one hand on the counter and held her glass in the other. Her vibrant blue eyes gave him a puzzled look —but she didn't back away.

"Why aren't you afraid of me?" he asked.

"Should I be?"

Seth didn't like the idea how Vanessa took a stranger in so willingly, or gave him food and shelter so readily. That she'd done so was the only reason he was still alive, but he couldn't rationalize her actions against his illogical fear that if she'd done the same for anyone else, they might have taken advantage of her—emotionally, financially, or even physically.

He scowled as he towered over her. "You're not taking your own safety seriously."

"I saved your life." She met his gaze.

"But you're not protecting your *own* life." His voice shifted to a low growl, but Vanessa seemed unfazed. Where was her sense of self-preservation? "You had a wounded man in your house—who you knew nothing about. You should've had your gun loaded and with you. Instead, you put him in your bedroom *with* your gun."

"You weren't in any position to attack anyone last night." Her voice stayed calm—not defensive or tentative.

"Then, you had the Sheriff at your house, and you didn't report a dangerous stranger just twenty feet away."

Without breaking eye contact, Vanessa arched an eyebrow and sipped her wine. "Do you always talk about yourself in the third person? Is that another quirk—like the intermittent Spanish?"

"Vanessa, I'm being serious."

"I realize that."

"You need to be more careful."

"From the average jerk, sure. You're a DEA agent and injured in the line of duty."

"Any well-intentioned law enforcement officer can become another creature in the throes of undercover work."

"Well, I don't see a dangerous creature in front of me."

Wasn't he? Vanessa didn't know him—not really. She didn't know the things Seth had done to rise through the ranks of Julio's hierarchy.

Seth gripped the counter on either side of her as he stared into her face. She truly wasn't afraid of him. How was that possible? Instead, her pupils were dilated and her lips parted. He pressed his body closer to hers until he felt her heart beating as fast as his own. Touching bodies, he knew Vanessa could feel his arousal. Still, those steady blue eyes of hers held not an ounce of fear. Only desire.

Seth couldn't remember the last time an unselfish woman had looked at him with raw desire. He leaned closer, certain she'd turn him away with scornful reproach at any moment—caution and self-preservation kicking in.

Before their lips touched, he caught sight of Vanessa's roses.

Right.

Boyfriend.

Seth leaned back as his fervor cooled. He wouldn't be the jerk who broke up the relationship of a woman who so selflessly helped him. He opened his mouth to apologize as he took a step back from her.

Vanessa turned away, her voice frosty. "Goodnight." Taking her glass of wine with her, Vanessa gave a short, sharp whistle, and Crick leaped to his feet to follow her into the bedroom. "I'll be keeping that gun close by." She closed the door.

Seth deflated with an exhalation. Vanessa was right to be angry with him. Somehow, his attempt to intimidate her—just to prove a point—had transformed into his wanting to seduce her.

Rico appeared beside him, looking toward the door. "You almost kissed her, *hombre*."

"I know," Seth grumbled. He began to wash the dishes. "I don't know what happened."

"She's pissed at you."

"Yeah, I got that vibe. It's a good thing I stopped when I did."

Rico laughed, a high-pitched cackle Seth had always found amusing. "She's pissed because you *didn't* kiss her."

"What? No, she's not. She has a boyfriend! She's pissed I came on to her. You'll see. In the morning, she'll be grateful."

"Yeah, we'll see about that, *Romeo*." Rico continued to laugh.

CHAPTER 5

*V*anessa woke the next morning to the smell of eggs and coffee. She'd slept heavily, but it had taken her an hour to cool the heat coursing through her—partly from arousal, partly from fury.

Seth made all that effort to get close to her and entice her—only to stop abruptly and with a look of such immense regret he might as well have dumped ice water over her head. What game was he playing?

Despite his initial efforts, she didn't feel the least bit intimidated by Seth. Having worked in an inner-city emergency room, she knew how to spot dangerous men. Seth probably was a dangerous DEA agent, but he wasn't a danger to her.

She seemed to realize, before he had, that his proximity was causing attraction to simmer inside her, not fear. By that time, the only fear she'd felt was that if she reached for him, she wouldn't be able to take her hands off him again.

Then, he'd stopped and backed off.

After the initial sting of rejection had worn off, Vanessa's rational mind realized he'd done the right thing. What would've happened if they'd kissed? A mediocre one-night stand? After which he'd have left to deal with his spider drug cartel—before finally slinking back into the shadows of a dual identity?

Vanessa had already endured a relationship that had diverged due to different career paths.

'What'd you think, Vanessa? That we'd grow old rocking on a ranch porch listening to George Strait? I'm destined for greater things. You could've been too..."

The words of her former fiancé had stung—as if choosing to be a rural family practitioner somehow meant choosing to be less.

Vanessa emerged from her bedroom, dressed and ready for her workday. She planned to breeze past Seth on her way out the door and avoid any awkward moments.

She unplugged her electronics and packed her medical bag.

"Sleep okay?"

When she turned, Seth stood beside her holding up a cup of coffee—cream, no sugar.

"Yes, thanks." She accepted the cup and drank.

"I made breakfast burritos."

Vanessa glanced at her watch as her stomach gave a perfectly timed growl. "I guess I have time to eat."

They sat at the kitchen table—Seth with one leg propped up in a chair at Vanessa's insistence. She noted that her gun was back out, placed conspicuously on the kitchen table.

"I'll check your bandages tonight."

"You have house calls today?"

"Yes. I took your advice and cancelled clinics. I can't do that indefinitely, though. When do you think your team will capture Julio?"

"I sent my boss an email yesterday. I need to place a follow-up phone call today…" His voice trailed off.

"But you don't have a phone. I'll pick one up for you."

"I should go with you."

"No, you shouldn't. You don't want to ride around on my house calls all day. You'd have to wait in the car— patient privacy and all that. I used to have to wait in the car on summer days when my mom was showing clients' properties for sale. Very dull."

"Let's call it protection duty. I've put you in danger, and I'm uncomfortable with it."

Vanessa bent around the table and looked pointedly at Seth's leg, eyes sparkling. "You're going to protect me like *that*?"

"I know how to watch for danger."

"Unlike me?" Vanessa's eyes flickered to the gun before she leveled her gaze back toward him.

"I'm sorry about last night."

She looked away and ate her burrito. How could she accept an apology when she didn't know what it was for? Was he sorry for insulting her ability to identify danger? Was he sorry for turning her on? Was he sorry for not finishing what he'd started?

Vanessa couldn't ask him these questions without revealing her vulnerability about the way he'd made her feel.

"Fine," she eventually snorted. "Tag along—but you need to be in the backseat where you can keep your leg propped up."

VANESSA ATTENDED her first house call uneventfully. Mr. Files was a man in his seventies, whom she treated for chronic obstructive pulmonary disease. She checked on him monthly, and each time she came he asked her why he felt short of breath. Each time, she'd had to patiently explain the pathophysiology of COPD and how his was related to fifty years of smoking cigarettes. If he quit smoking, he could prevent further deterioration of his breathing. Each time, he gave her a condescending look over his glasses.

"Doctor, I'm seventy years old. Why do you want me to stop the only thing in life I still enjoy?"

Having finished her exam, Vanessa packed up her medical bag. "What kind of doctor would I be if I didn't give you medical advice?"

Mr. Files picked his novel up from the end table beside the recliner where he sat. "When will you be back?"

"One month?"

"I'll see you then." He didn't look up from his book.

Vanessa smiled as she let herself out of his house. Mr. Files pretended not to enjoy her visits, but he always wanted to know when she would return.

She opened the car door and set the medical bag in the front passenger seat.

"Do you always smile at the end of patient visits?" Seth asked.

She buckled in and started the engine. "I don't know. I've never had someone point it out to me. This patient is a crotchety old man who can't help but like me. It makes me smile."

"You seem to deeply enjoy your job."

She drove off the driveway and onto a country road. "I surely do. I refuse to work at something I don't enjoy."

"Sounds like you're speaking from experience."

"Yes, well—when a family is screaming at you that they'll sue you if their grandbaby doesn't survive its delivery, after the mom used illegal drugs during pregnancy and had no prenatal care, it's hard to enjoy saving lives."

"Inner city ER?"

"Yes."

"You left to be happier?"

"Yes."

"Did you leave anything or any*one* behind?"

Vanessa thought about Mitchel as she drove the back roads of rural Texas. She hadn't left her former fiancé behind. She'd taken an opportunity, and he'd declined to follow her. She decided to let Seth's question go.

"What about you?" Vanessa asked. "Are you happy as an undercover DEA agent?"

"Happiness isn't the point of what I do."

"You must have some sort of intrinsic reward." She glanced in the rearview mirror at Seth. He gazed out the window with a hand on his chin. Even his profile was handsome—defined jaw, tapered nose, and long, thick lashes.

"When I take down Julio, I'll enjoy it. But you evaded my question."

"Why do you assume I left something behind? Maybe I just left."

"You're an intelligent, beautiful woman living alone. There's more to your story."

"Maybe I *like* living alone."

"Maybe you do, but it doesn't mean you've always been alone."

"Everyone has a past."

"That they do," he said. "Are you running from something?"

"No, Seth. Unlike you, I have no secret identity. I wanted to have a quiet, rural life—practicing medicine on a personal level with my patients. My fiancé wanted to be an surgeon in a busy urban practice. We parted ways amicably at the end of our residency. Here I am."

SETH DETECTED in Vanessa's tone that 'amicably' didn't mean without heartache. He probably shouldn't have pushed Vanessa so hard, but he needed a logical explanation for her isolation. If she was hiding from someone, it would only escalate the problem he'd created in her life with Julio.

"That was how long ago?"

"A year."

"I'm sorry. He's an idiot."

"You don't even know him."

"He let you go. That's proof enough of his idiocy."

Vanessa chuckled. "Thanks."

"If it's any consolation, I'd be dead if you had decided to stay with Idiot."

"His name is Mitchel."

"I'm going to stick with Idiot."

Vanessa laughed again, a musical sound Seth deeply enjoyed. She pulled down a gravel driveway and parked her car. She unplugged the phone she'd bought him and handed it over.

"It's fully charged."

Their hands brushed as he took the phone. He couldn't see her expression, but he felt the tingle of electricity dance through his hand.

As she exited the car to see her next patient, Seth frowned. The dilapidated wooden home looked sketchy. Shingles were missing on the roof, and the windows looked like they hadn't seen any window-cleaner since their installation fifty years ago.

"I've seen drug deals go down in establishments like that."

Rico materialized in the front passenger seat. "Me too, *hombre*—but even drug dealers need doctors," he offered helpfully.

Seth grunted as she disappeared into the house. "I guess she's not really mine to worry about." He thought again about the sheriff. Perhaps Gregg was the sort of man Vanessa needed. Few people would be reckless enough to endanger the wife of the County Sheriff.

Wife. The idea had Seth battling an absurd pang of jealousy.

"She could be yours to worry about—if you wanted," Rico said.

Seth dialed his boss's number on his phone. "I have work to do." The sooner Julio was dealt with, the sooner Seth could extricate himself from Vanessa's life.

Rico faded into the seat.

"Agent Green."

"It's Seth."

"*Dammit*, Dellosa, I got your email. Are you okay? Because if you're okay, I'm going to have your ass for this. I've got a dead Federale and two dead civilians."

"Civilians?"

"*Las Arañas* is tearing up half of Texas looking for you. Can you come in?"

"Soon. I need a little more time to heal from a bullet wound before I come in and Julio finds me." Seth rubbed a hand over his jeans above the bandage on his leg.

"Come in. We'll take care of you."

"I'd like that—I really would—but as soon as the DEA knows where I am, Julio will know. I need to keep lying low just a little longer."

"What are you implying, Dellosa?" Jody's tone hardened.

"Somebody ratted out Rico Valez. Because I don't know who or where the mole is, I'm not exposing myself."

"Can you at least send us everything you have on Julio? The Chief of Operations is on me to make sure your last five years weren't a complete waste."

"The notes I have are in my head. It's not as though I could have stored everything somewhere traceable. I'll work on getting them on file to you, but…"

Seth suddenly heard the sound of tires on gravel. When he turned, the sheriff's car pulled into view.

Crap.

CHAPTER 6

*D*amn, this man is tenacious.

"I gotta go." Seth hung up the phone. He stuffed it into his jeans pocket and exited the car. After closing the passenger door, he leaned against the car for support—and to give the appearance of casual innocence. He suppressed a grimace as his leg protested his quick movements.

The blond-haired sheriff exited his cruiser and placed his Stetson on his head. For a country lawman, he had nothing rugged in his appearance. If he hadn't had a pistol on his hip, he could easily have been a Boy Scout troop leader. Maybe he'd been one before signing up as a law officer. Still, Seth could imagine Vanessa endeared to Gregg's boyish, wholesome good looks.

"Sheriff," Seth greeted him with a nod.

"Welcome to town. I don't recognize you. You new here?" The Sheriff smiled as he casually looped his thumbs through his belt.

Seth had the urge to tap into the southern twang he'd

learned growing up in Texas and answer, *'I ain't from 'round these parts'*—but he didn't think Gregg would appreciate the joke.

"Just passing through. Visiting with Dr. Watson." Seth extended a hand. "Seth Dellosa."

"Gregg Child." He seemed to warm at Seth referring to Vanessa as Dr. Watson, probably because it suggested a professional rather than personal relationship.

They shook hands.

That Gregg would feel relief at the idea Seth and Vanessa were on formal terms hinted that the depth of their relationship—especially since Vanessa had no pictures of her and Gregg together in her home—was either insecure or in its infancy.

"How do you know Vanessa?" Gregg asked.

The door of the house opened, and Vanessa started toward them.

Seth raised his hands slowly, defensively. "We're just friends, Sheriff."

Vanessa saw his motions and hurried to them. "What's going on?"

At her alarmed voice, Seth felt a jolt of surprise at Vanessa coming to his defense.

"Gregg, are you following me?" Vanessa asked.

Seth lowered his hands and leaned back against the car, suppressing a grin. Vanessa apparently didn't appreciate an overprotective boyfriend.

"I wasn't following you. My deputy informed me he saw you driving with plastic over your back windshield and someone in your back seat. There've been two murders reported in the county west of here, so I wanted to check on you. I called Kailee and asked where you were." He spoke slowly and calmly, probably a tone he'd learned to use when dealing with angry parishioners.

"I have a phone."

"Which you didn't answer."

Vanessa pulled it out of her pocket and looked at it. "I must have poor service here."

"Hence, my presence."

Her cheeks flushed pink. "Okay, well, thank you, Gregg. I'm fine. We've got one more stop to make."

Gregg's eye twitched at the word 'we'.

Yes, definitely some insecurity between them.

"What happened to your rear window?"

"Oh." Vanessa gave a nervous chuckle. "Yeah, it shattered." She shifted her weight and tugged a wayward strand of red hair behind her ear. "Scared the hell out of me."

Seth pursed his lips. She was still protecting him and yet seemed incapable of lying. How refreshing. He'd spent the last five years in a world of liars and scoundrels. He'd been one of them.

Vanessa glanced back at the house before squaring her shoulders at Gregg. "I think you're scaring my patient. She keeps looking through her curtains."

Gregg tipped his hat at Vanessa before turning back to Seth. "And your name again?"

"Seth…"

"I'm going to the Valentine's dance," Vanessa blurted out the words.

Gregg's lips parted in a smile. "You are?"

"Yes. I'll see you there?"

Gregg's smile widened. "I'll see you there!"

As if rejuvenated, Gregg walked back to his cruiser with a lightness in his step. He finally drove away.

She exhaled and turned to Seth. "You! Back in the car."

"There's a town Valentine's dance?"

"Music, beer, baked goods. It's a small-town thing, right?"

"You're going stag to the Valentine's dance?"

She bristled. "It seems so. Let's go."

He obliged, watching her flustered expression and flushed cheeks.

SETH LET Vanessa stew in silence as she drove. He wasn't sure what had set off her temper, but he guessed the predicament he'd put her in by arriving in a hailstorm of violence and then tagging along with her had played a significant role. He was also clearly interfering with something between her and Gregg.

Vanessa pulled into a gas station ten minutes into the drive and checked her phone. "The last patient cancelled, so I'll take you straight home." She pulled back onto the road, looking more defeated now than angry.

Two patient visits a day probably wouldn't pay any bills. He needed to let her life get back to normal. "I'm sorry, Vanessa. Give me this week—just two more days—and I'll be out of your hair."

"Marvelous." Her voice sounded flat.

He shook his head in frustration. He wished he was sitting beside her, where he could at least read her expression. If his leaving didn't bring her relief, then that suggested she wasn't upset about his intrusion. But if she wasn't upset about the intrusion, what *was* she upset about?

"Do you want to talk about why you're upset?"

"Not particularly."

VANESSA COULDN'T ARTICULATE why she felt angry, because she wasn't entirely sure herself. She didn't like the scene earlier, where Seth had stood backed up against her car like a criminal, while Gregg looked at him like he was about to interrogate Seth. Why did she feel protective of a DEA agent?

She didn't like that Gregg was 'checking up on her' either—even though his rationale made perfect sense. She wasn't his to protect.

Furthermore, she also felt annoyed that when the idea to attend the Valentine dance had popped into her head, she'd wanted to say she was attending *with Seth*. And yet, she hardly knew the man.

All of her irrational behavior and emotions fed the fire of Vanessa's frustration. She normally prided herself on *not* having a stereotypical redheaded temper—but being around Seth seemed to stoke the flames of irritation and frustration.

"Are you upset about Gregg? Did I screw up your relationship?"

"Don't flatter yourself. And we don't have a relationship."

"Of course we don't."

"No. I mean, *Gregg and I* aren't a couple. We're not dating. We've been on *one* date."

"Oh. So, the Valentine dance was to distract him from me?"

"Yeah. You need to maintain a low profile, right? Your life—and mine—depend on it, right?"

"You otherwise weren't planning to go to this function?" His voice sounded contrite.

She glanced back at him. It was hard to stay angry when Seth sounded so concerned. "It's nothing. It's one social event."

"Still—you owe me nothing. You didn't have to do that."

"If I hadn't, it would've been a marathon of questions: 'How do you know Vanessa?' 'Where are you from?' 'Where are you heading?' Then, there'd be lying."

"You don't like lying."

"I abhor lying." She pulled into her driveway.

Crick stood on the porch, wagging his tail. Vanessa grabbed her medical bag as Seth struggled out of the back seat.

"Do you need me to help you up the stairs?" Vanessa asked.

"Just as far as the railing. Once I have something to lean on, I can manage."

She wrapped one arm around him as Seth put his left arm over her shoulder. His body felt warm and firm—and smelled like sandalwood with a dash of vanilla. He'd used her soap, she realized.

After she helped him up the steps and all the way inside her house, she was fully aware she didn't want to take her hands off him until she absolutely had to. She eased him onto the couch, wishing for one irrational moment that he'd pull her down on top of him like he had the other night.

'We don't have a relationship.'

'Of course we don't.'

Such plain truth. So, why did she feel a pull toward Seth? A desire to protect him, hold him, and feel his touch?

Vanessa lifted her laptop from the table. "I have some more work to do." She went to her room and closed the door behind her.

In addition to clinic and house calls, she did ten hours of chart reviews per week for an insurance company. After propping up the pillows on her bed, Vanessa sat and opened her laptop to work.

A KNOCK SOUNDED on Vanessa's door. "Come in."

Seth opened the door, balancing a tray of drinks. She hopped up to help.

"I thought you might need something. I just wasn't sure which drink you'd prefer, so I brought them all— water, juice, and hot tea."

She took the tray. "Oh. Thank you."

He limped back out of her room, closing the door behind him. She set the tray down and started with tea while it was still hot.

Over the next hour, Vanessa drank her way through each of the beverages as she worked on the chart reviews.

When she finished, she emerged from the room, carrying the tray of empty glasses to the kitchen.

"What's that smell?" Vanessa breathed in the scent of garlic and basil.

"Chicken."

"You're cooking dinner?"

"Is that okay?"

"Yes, I've just never had a man in my kitchen cooking dinner for me before."

Like cooking her breakfast, there was an intimacy to the act of having someone in her home cooking dinner for her. She liked that he had this nurturing side to him.

"You never had a brother cook for you?"

"No brothers." She hesitated before adding, "I'm an only child."

"What about the surgeon you dated?" Seth poured wine and water into glasses on an already prepared table.

She gave him a puzzled look. "He had siblings."

"No." Seth grinned. "He never cooked for you?"

"Oh, no. We both worked eighty-hour weeks. Dinner usually consisted of takeout."

Vanessa walked to the oven and clicked on the internal light. "It looks delicious!"

"Baked salsa chicken."

"So, is your caramel skin, Spanish second language, and Mexican cooking from heritage, or being undercover?"

Seth grabbed oven mitts and took the chicken out of the oven. "My mother is an immigrant from Cuernavaca. My father was an American businessman who met her during his travels. They've been happily married for fifty years. Five children." Seth carried the pan to the table and set it on a trivet.

Vanessa cringed at his limp. "You're pushing it on your feet, Seth."

"I'm not an invalid."

She thought about the muscular torso she'd seen bare the other night. "No, you're not—but I don't want you bleeding through *my* bandages or tearing *my* stitches. I worked hard on those. I'll finish carrying everything else to the table."

JULIO RECLINED on the balcony of his hotel room. Waiting to hear back from Val on the status of the traitor felt agonizingly interminable. The time gave Julio too much opportunity to reflect back on the many moments he'd spent with Seth, never knowing the traitor's true identity.

Julio had even offered a cigar to Jorge—the traitor he'd later learn was named Seth. Seth had green eyes and kept a thick beard all year round. The fullness of it was the envy of some of Julio's men—who themselves could grow uneven patches of facial hair at best.

Seth had taken the cigar.

After Julio lit the cigars, they'd both smoked. Julio had ordered Val to pour them both a single malt whiskey to complement their cigars as the two of them had sat on the balcony of Julio's estate outside Mexico City.

"You handled the González brothers well," Julio remarked.

"They won't steal from you again." Seth sipped the whiskey.

Julio had admired the man's calm demeanor. Seth could stare down armed gunmen with the same cool detachment with which he drank his whisky. Nothing seemed to faze Seth—standoffs, guns, knives, or even being outnumbered. Nothing.

"They're still alive, though." Julio calmly puffed out his cigar, judging Seth's reaction from the corner of his eye. "I said dead."

"You did. You also taught me that living thieves are more useful than dead ones. Now, you won't be short men for the Tijuana delivery."

At that time, when Seth was still the trusted Jorge to Julio, he'd thought of Seth as such a clever right-hand man. So calculating—just like himself. In hindsight, Julio couldn't recall Seth ever having killed anyone. He'd been a formidable fighter and indispensable consultant about the drug trafficking business—but he'd never murdered anybody, even if they'd deserved it. Perhaps that should have been a red flag, but Julio had honestly believed this to be part of Seth's ruthless calculations.

Regardless, Julio would now fix his mistake. Seth couldn't hide forever.

CHAPTER 7

*S*eth didn't mind watching Vanessa walk back and forth from the kitchen to the table. Her hair was pulled back into a haphazard updo, with loose strands of red sticking out and flowing as she moved.

Dinner with a beautiful woman gave him a pleasant distraction from the business of dealing with *Las Arañas*. He'd used Vanessa's laptop, typed up about half of everything he knew, and sent a preliminary report to his boss. When he'd made a follow-up call to ensure Jody had received the email, he'd given Seth an update. Julio still had not been located. He could be back in Mexico—or he could be planning his assault on Seth at that very moment. Seth had sent Rico's spirit to do reconnaissance, but his friend hadn't returned yet.

When the food was served, Seth and Vanessa ate sitting across from each other at the table.

Seth motioned to a workbook on Vanessa's counter. "You're learning Spanish?"

"I'm deep in the heart of Texas. I need to know it down here. *Yo estoy practicando.*"

"Very nice."

"I still don't know half of what you said the other night. You spoke fast and quietly. Are you aware that when you talk to yourself, you do so in Spanish?" She drank a sip of wine.

"I don't talk to myself."

"You do—I've heard you. Even if I discount the night you were shot, bleeding, and delirious, I heard you earlier today from my room."

Seth set down his fork. He could've lied—could've told her he was talking on the phone. But he wanted Vanessa to know the truth—his truth. Maybe if she judged him for it, then leaving her when the time came would be easier.

"What you heard wasn't a conversation with myself."

Vanessa blinked at him, wineglass in hand. "Talking to your demons then?"

"Talking to my partner—Rico."

"I thought you said Julio killed him."

"He did."

She finished her glass of wine. "You're honestly going to give me your most serious expression while telling me —*what*? That you talk to your dead partner's ghost?"

He braced for her fury, but none came. Either she'd burned through her reserve for the day, or the wine had chilled it.

She continued, "Well, you're an otherwise rational man. Perhaps the stress you've been through is manifesting as hallucinations. With medication and counseling…"

"I'm not hallucinating, Vanessa. I've had the gift of interacting with spirits ever since I was sixteen. My mother has it. Some of my siblings have it."

Vanessa appraised him keen eyes. "You're telling me this because…"

"…because you abhor lies. I don't want to lie to you."

She shook her head, her voice remaining calm, almost weary. "No. This isn't you telling the truth. This is some type of distancing technique."

"I cooked you dinner, and I'm not leaving until Julio is dealt with. I'm not distancing."

Seth could have told her that Rico was how he'd discovered her gun and her password. He could have summoned Rico and made him tell Seth something he'd otherwise have no way of knowing—like the name of the first boy Vanessa had kissed, or her score on the medical college admissions test.

But such a display would probably put her off more than she already was.

Vanessa gave Seth a resigned look before finishing her salsa chicken. Then she stood and cleared the table.

Brilliant idea, Seth scolded himself.

Before he'd pushed out of his chair, keeping the weight on his right leg, she'd already moved all the dishes from the table to the kitchen sink. He stood beside her at the sink and helped her wash the dishes.

Based on the red splotches creeping up her neck, her irritation with him was mounting. He smiled at the significance of her feelings—if Vanessa didn't care about him, she wouldn't care if he'd claimed to see ghosts or was 'distancing' himself.

He stared out the large window over the sink as he rinsed the dishes, handing them to her one-by-one for the dishwasher. "How much of the land do you own?"

"Just beyond the tree line."

"Must be ten acres out there."

She looked wistfully at the cleared pastureland. "That's right."

"Are you planning something with all of that space?"

"I want a house—not a rickety shack like this. And I want a large garden, and maybe a pool."

"That's only one tenth of the space."

"Sometimes, I think horses would be nice."

"Have you ever owned a horse?"

"No. But my dad took me on a trail ride in Montana—one of the touristy ones. It seemed so peaceful. Horse, rider, and nature."

Seth pictured Vanessa riding a horse, wearing leather boots and a cowgirl hat.

"Have you ever ridden?"

"Yeah. I had friends with horses growing up, and I rode with them. I can see the appeal of a busy physician wanting moments of tranquility."

She reached toward him for another dish, but Seth took her hand instead. "That's all of them."

She looked at their hands, clasped together, as her throat moved up and down in a swallow. Did she feel as lightheaded at his touch as he did at hers?

"Vanessa…"

"No. I'm not some woman you seduce on your way out of town—and I'm not contracting some STD you picked up in a Mexican brothel. I'm nobody's one-night stand."

He laughed. He knew Vanessa was serious—so laughing would probably piss her off—but he couldn't help himself.

She jerked her hand back and stared at his audacity.

Amused, he leaned on the counter. "First of all, we've already established I'm not leaving."

"Yet."

"Secondly, I've never been in a brothel, and I've only slept with one woman in the last five years. Next, I don't have any sexually transmitted diseases—and lastly, did your mind seriously go straight to sex? All I hoped for was a kiss. So, you tell *me*, Dr. Watson, who in this relationship needs to be more worried about being taken advantage of?"

Speechless, Vanessa's mouth gaped as her cheeks burned red.

"I…" She lowered her head—and then finally laughed. "You're absolutely right. I went directly off the deep end."

"If it's any consolation, I'm flattered."

"I'm partly consoled and partly mortified." She poured another glass of wine.

"Would you be wholly consoled if we platonically watched a movie? Your pick."

She glanced over her shoulder with a devious grin as she walked toward the living room. "Damn right it's my pick. It's my house."

Seth laughed, relishing her spunk. He followed her into the living room.

~

VANESSA SAT on the opposite end of the sofa from Seth, and they enjoyed *The Princess Bride* together. Crick laid on the couch between them and put his head in Vanessa's lap. She was pleasantly surprised when Seth told her he'd seen the movie a dozen times, and that it ranked in his top ten for romantic comedies.

She'd wanted to kiss Seth in the kitchen—but, in her anger, pushed him away instead. But she'd done the right thing, because any intimacy would only make her miss him more when he inevitably left.

Relaxing into the movie, she set aside Seth's strange claim to see ghosts. She'd seen her share of delusional patients, and Seth didn't fit the profile. She recalled another instance of a seemingly normal person claiming to see ghosts.

The pleasant, seventy-five-year-old Louisa had been admitted to the hospital with uncontrolled atrial fibrillation. Vanessa had been on an inpatient rotation during residency and fixed the woman's rapid heart rate. She'd had multiple conversations with her patient about her life as a teacher, and her children and grandchildren.

On the day of her hospital discharge, Louisa had asked Vanessa, "Have you ever wondered why butterflies land on you when you're outside?"

Vanessa cocked her head to one side. "How did you know...?"

"It's Alex."

Vanessa felt a chill spread down her spine. "What?"

"I see and hear spirits, and Alex told me he sends his love to you in the form of butterflies. He's very proud of you and the life you've made."

Tears pricked Vanessa's eyes. Alex had been her still-born twin—a brother she'd only known in the womb, and yet a sense of loss had always followed her like a small, hovering rain cloud. She'd always wished him a happy birthday on her own birthday.

Vanessa had filed Louisa's words in the bizarre, inexplicable folder of her memory—but a week later, had nevertheless driven the three hours to Alex's grave; where she was reminded of the butterfly etched in the granite beneath his name. As Vanessa had sat on the cool, soft grass, she'd felt the familiar weight of guilt that she lived and Alex hadn't. A butterfly had then landed on her shoulder, bringing Vanessa to a body-wrenching cathartic cry and her own forgiveness.

Back in the present, the movie ended, and Vanessa looked over to see that Seth had fallen asleep. She coaxed Crick off the couch and eased Seth into a more comfortable position, occupying the entire couch. She covered him with an afghan before going to her own room to prepare for bed.

CHAPTER 8

The next morning, Vanessa woke with renewed resolve. She'd finish a half-day of work and then finally sort out what Seth needed to move on. She was entirely too comfortable with him in her house, cooking meals and watching movies.

She exited her room dressed and ready for work in slacks and a buttoned blouse. Seth had coffee waiting. She packed up her medical bag and then requested Seth sit to inspect his bandages.

"We're off to work after this?" Seth asked.

"*I'm* off to work. You're off that leg."

"Vanessa…"

"It's been two days, Seth, and Julio hasn't found us yet. I'll be fine."

"I disagree."

She cut off the old bandage and inspected the wound. It was healing without evidence of infection. "You can puff your chest out all you want. Besides, I don't need you

77

and Gregg making Clint Eastwood eyes at each other again."

Seth's lips quirked. "Clint Eastwood eyes?"

"You know what I mean." Vanessa wrapped his leg in a clean bandage.

"You're not going without me."

"You and what army is going to force me to take you with me?" She inspected the cut on his arm she sutured, but it didn't need a dressing change.

Seth crossed his arms. She busied herself drinking her coffee so as not to betray how attractive she found him playing Mr. Protective. And why was he attractive with this behavior while she found it annoying in Gregg? Probably because Seth approached her like an equal, and Gregg's concern felt more like he was looking out for the helpless little missus.

"At least take the gun," Seth said.

"What if you need it?"

Seth grinned. "If you're worried about *me*, take me with you."

Vanessa bit her lip. Was Seth in more danger by staying at her house? Or accompanying her?

"I'll be vulnerable here—trapped and wounded." His eyes became doleful as his bottom lip protruded.

Vanessa blinked at him. Even with a bullet wound, he hardly looked trapped and wounded.

"You're unbelievable," she grumbled.

"You wouldn't abandon a helpless man."

She struggled to suppress a smile, not wanting to encourage him. "Fine. Get in the car."

He snatched his coffee and followed her to the car. His

movements turned swift and fluid as he suppressed his limp.

"Helpless man my ass," she said, grinning wryly as she got into the car.

Seth made an obvious effort to look at her backside.

She rolled her eyes, but couldn't suppress a smile. "Is there anything I can say to *not* encourage you?"

"Probably not." His tone was cheerful—that of a man high on victory.

ON THE ROAD BETWEEN PATIENTS, Vanessa and Seth compared favorite movies and favorite songs. He told her about his siblings, while she confided in him about Alex. She even went as far as to tell him about Louisa's claim—and how it gave her a happy thrill to think of Alex sending her butterflies.

He smiled with a distant look in his eyes. He didn't use the conversation to bring up his dead friend.

When her assistant called, Vanessa answered the phone. "Hey, Kailee."

"What's your twenty?"

"Three thirty-nine and two eighty-three. Why?"

"The Coramond family called. Maxwell's having shortness of breath and chest pain. They sound really panicked—like whatever it is, it could be life-threatening."

"Maxwell? He's only twenty, right?" Vanessa had met Maxwell when he'd brought his mother to her clinic appointment, but Vanessa hadn't treated him previously.

"Right. They said they'd brought him to the clinic, but they called me when they saw it was closed."

"Did you tell them to call an ambulance?"

"Yes, they're doing it now."

"Okay. Thanks, Kailee. I'm turning around. I can meet them at my clinic in three minutes." Vanessa turned off the call. "Hold on," she told Seth, making a quick U-turn before accelerating down the highway.

"Can you prep my bag for me?" she asked.

Seth pulled her bag from the back seat onto his lap. "What do you need?"

"Maxwell is tall and lanky. My first guess is a pneumothorax—air in the chest cavity, collapsing his lung. Of course, best case scenario is he's just suffering a vicious case of reflux."

"What's the worst-case scenario?"

"A blood clot. I don't have anything to treat a pulmonary embolism."

"So, we hope for reflux—but prepare for lung collapse?"

"Exactly. I need my ultrasound probe ready to go."

Seth shuffled through the bag. "Okay. It's on top and powered on."

"Thanks."

When she pulled into her clinic parking lot, she spotted the Coramond's car immediately. Tossing her medical bag over her shoulder, she got out of her car and walked to their vehicle, where Maxwell sat in the back seat.

"What happened?" Vanessa asked.

The boy's frantic mother paced the asphalt and

chewed her nails. "He just started hurting and couldn't breathe. Please help him."

Maxwell clutched his chest while his breath came short and fast. With her stethoscope, Vanessa listened for breathing sounds. None could be auscultated on the right side of his chest. With his mother's help, they tugged off Maxwell's shirt.

Vanessa pulled out the ultrasound, applied lubricant, and pressed the probe to the right side of his chest, just beneath his collarbone.

An ambulance pulled into the parking lot at that moment, lights still flashing as they cut the sirens off. Two paramedics hopped out and strode rapidly around to the back of the big van, opening the rear doors to pull out a stretcher.

The ultrasound probe confirmed the presence of a pneumothorax.

She introduced herself as Dr. Watson before asking, "What do you have for a chest tube?" Vanessa squeezed lidocaine jelly onto a 4x4 gauze and placed it on a spot over his right chest.

"A trauma chest seal," the taller paramedic said.

"That'll work. Can you hand it to me?"

He left to fetch it while the other paramedic climbed into the opposite side of the car and took the patient's pulse and blood pressure. "You're the new family doc, aren't you?"

"That's me." She pulled on a pair of gloves and cleaned the area where the skin had absorbed the lidocaine. "What gave it away?"

"Not many redheads around here." He started working on an IV in Maxwell's left arm.

"Oh, I thought the request for a chest would've done it."

"Nah. There are a few veterans around here who know what a chest tube is. Say that's a fancy ultrasound you've got there."

"I don't leave home without it."

The other paramedic brought the chest seal over and peeled open the container.

Vanessa picked it out of the wrapper. "I'm sorry, Maxwell. The lidocaine has numbed the surface, but this is going to hurt like getting kicked in the chest by a mule." Vanessa had never been kicked by an animal, but she'd heard stories—and it seemed like an appropriate analogy for a country boy.

Maxwell nodded, still diaphoretic and gasping for air.

With the IV secured, the paramedic pushed a dose of morphine into the IV tubing. He turned and began applying EKG leads.

Vanessa applied pressure to insert the chest seal between Maxwell's ribs and into his chest cavity. As Maxwell screamed, she felt it pop through. Air audibly escaped through the one-way valve. Maxwell's head rolled back as he fainted. The monitor held a steady heartbeat.

"It's just a vagal response to the pain. He'll be okay," she told his mother. Backing out of the car, Vanessa gave the paramedics room to move the patient to the stretcher.

As she walked back to her car, she stretched the kinks out of her neck from working in such an awkward position when treating Maxwell. In hindsight, she probably should have gotten help pulling him out of the vehicle but she hadn't wanted to delay the chest tube.

Seth leaned on the car, having watched the entire emergency scene unfold. "Another life saved," he said. "That's two in one week."

Vanessa nodded to him, pulling off her gloves with a snap and reaching back to sweep her hair from her sweating neck. She'd gotten hot working in the back seat of the Coramond's car. Thank heavens it was February and not July.

"I need to go with Maxwell to the hospital."

"I'll tag along in your car and pick you up."

"You're okay to drive?"

"Yeah."

"Okay. The nearest hospital is Corpus Christi Hospital. It's illegal to follow an ambulance, and the last thing you need is to get pulled over, so take your time." Vanessa paused. "Why are you grinning?"

"With all of this going on," he gestured to the Coramond's care and the ambulance, "you're still worried about me?"

Vanessa leaned forward and patted Seth's cheek. "You're under my protection, remember?"

SETH FOLLOWED the GPS on his phone to the hospital. His cheek still felt warm from Vanessa's touch.

The physician in action had amazed him. In and out of consciousness and doped on narcotics just two nights earlier, he hadn't been able to watch her fix him. Seeing her save that kid's life just now, though, filled Seth with awe.

Here was a woman so dedicated to her craft that she didn't hesitate in helping those in need, and yet she remained as cool as *horchata* under pressure. He bet she'd taste just as sweet.

Seth drove past the ER bay of the hospital, where the ambulance that had collected Maxwell was parked. He suspected Vanessa would need a few minutes with the ER physician, so Seth decided to use the time to do some quick shopping. He pulled into a strip mall across the street from the hospital.

"Seth?"

Seth jumped slightly as Rico appeared. "*Hijole!* You scared me, Rico. Hang on." Accustomed to speaking with ghosts in public, Seth found his phone and pretended to speak into it. Talking to Rico with a mobile phone pressed against his ear made him look less crazy to the casual observer.

He put the phone to his ear as he walked into the store. "You were gone a while. I got worried."

The building angst in Rico's absence felt like a bad omen, but Seth's worry subsided now that his former partner was back. Ghosts were usually good about tracking down people they knew, but time worked differently for apparitions—so a day for the living didn't always correspond to a day for a spirit.

"The DEA is clean. A Federale ratted on me." Rico's voice held disdain. "That's how Julio found out I was undercover. And why he didn't know about you until I told him."

"Okay. I need to make arrangements to have my boss bring me in tomorrow."

Jody Green could put some real protection on Vanessa —two uninjured agents—while Seth helped arrest efforts on Julio.

Rico nodded.

Seth dialed Jody's number.

On top of everything with his work, these budding feelings for Vanessa swelled like a rising tide. Based on her twinkling expressions and the quirk of her lips, the redhead was as interested in him as he was with her. His irrational feelings had Seth wanting to fix her dinner every night and coffee every morning, which was preposterous, because they'd only known each other a few days. Not to mention he couldn't build a quality relationship on this rocky foundation—him dropping into her car, bleeding and needing rescue.

Or, could he?

TWENTY MINUTES LATER, Seth pulled into the ER patient parking lot and approached the sliding glass door that read EMERGENCY ROOM. Vanessa exited, carrying a cane.

"I picked you up a gift."

He took the cane. "Thanks. How's the kid?"

"Good. He'll be fine. He's getting a real chest tube right now."

Seth put the cane in his left hand and gave her his right elbow. "Home?"

She hooked her arm through his. "Yes. I need a shower before the Valentine's dance."

With Vanessa back at the wheel, she drove them to her house.

"I've made arrangements to get picked up tomorrow by a DEA team. My boss will get a protection team on you until Julio is in custody."

"You've been busy." Vanessa didn't look at him, keeping her eyes fixed on the road ahead. The sound of the engine humming filled the gaping void Seth felt between them.

"I can't thank you enough for what you did for me. You saved my life." He knew he was repeating himself from the other day, but the silence felt agonizing.

"Don't mention it." Vanessa glanced back at Seth, this time with a playful curve to her lips. "Seriously, *don't mention it*. I don't need any Mexican drug dealers coming after me because I helped you."

Seth chuckled. He enjoyed her humor as much as her sass.

"It's good you're leaving. I've got a reservation at the indoor batting cage. The community softball league starts up in May, and I want to make a good impression my first time on their team. I can't practice if I'm running a shelter for injured DEA agents."

Seth sought the words to ask if he could call her sometime or stop by and see her, but all too soon, Vanessa was pulling into her driveway and hopping out of the car.

She pulled open the back seat, where Seth sat with his leg propped up. "Can I help you out?"

"I have the cane now, so I can manage. Thanks."

He watched her bound onto the porch and bend down

to greet Crick with a thorough petting. He wanted those hands on him.

Yes. He should have just said: *'Yes, I'd love to have your help.'*

~

JULIO ANSWERED the phone call from Val. "*Que pasa?*"

"We found the DEA agent. He showed up with a woman back at the clinic. Her car is missing the rear window, so she's the one who helped him escape. He's wounded and limping. I'm following them. She's got a real remote house, so I could probably take them both out right now."

Julio felt a cold lump in his chest, like an iron fist wrapping around his heart. Seth had betrayed him. They'd bonded—or so Julio had thought—over conversations about his family. He'd confided dreams and aspirations to Seth. The betrayal was like a knife wound.

Julio would *finish* him.

"No, stay on him and follow them if they go anywhere. Tonight, when the sky is darkest, you and I will kill the DEA agent *together.*"

CHAPTER 9

*V*anessa showered and donned a red dress. She hadn't worn a dress since—well, she couldn't even remember when. The color seemed bold, but red had to be appropriate for a Valentine's dance, right?

She fixed her hair down and straight and wore conservative one-inch heels.

When she emerged from her bedroom, she found Seth standing in the living room, waiting for her. He wore blue jeans, pairing them with a button shirt, and his hair was combed smooth.

Her ridiculous heart skipped a beat. Although the sentimental organ wouldn't anticipate the ache that would come when Seth left in the morning, Vanessa knew what was coming.

She crossed her arms. "Are we having this argument again? You need to stay here and let your leg heal." She shouldn't go either with the threat of Mexican drug dealers, but not going would have Gregg back at her door asking questions.

His eyes twinkled with mischief. "We had a *disagreement*, not an argument. And are you going to make me explain how vulnerable I am without you again?"

She turned and snatched her purse off the counter. "I can't even talk to you when you're like this."

"Charming?"

Biting her lip, she walked toward the door with Seth following along on his cane. "Yes, *maddeningly* charming—and knowing it."

"Um? Are you calling me arrogant? You wouldn't insult a guy with a cane, would you?" He followed her down the steps.

She reached for the door handle to her car, but Seth beat her to it. For a moment, as their hands touched, she felt warmth undulate through her.

"You're surprisingly fast for a man with a cane."

He opened the door for her. "I have many skills."

She swallowed and only broke eye contact to climb into the driver's seat. This time, Seth sat in the front passenger seat. His jaw tensed as he bent his knee to fit into the compact space.

"Did you take more ibuprofen?"

"Yes, doctor." Seth winked at her. "I'll be fine."

WHEN THEY REACHED the gardens where the Valentine festivities were being held, Vanessa parked her car and began making rounds—talking to the townspeople. Part of her success and acceptance as the local physician here hinged on being able to make people feel comfortable with her presence and build trust with them even though she was an outsider. Most people asked about her practice and how she liked the town. A few praised Vanessa for what they'd heard about Maxwell. News traveled swiftly through the small-town gossip stream.

While Vanessa socialized, Seth kept to the shadows. She sensed him watching her and wanted to ask who was protecting whom tonight.

As she conversed with the locals, she admired the pink and red Chinese lanterns and the decorative roses adorning all the booths and tables. Taco, burger, and barbecue vendors lined the periphery of the gardens. Booths sold heart-shaped sugar cookies, strawberry jam, and cupcakes decorated with pink icing. A concrete clearing in the middle of the gardens was prepped for dancing, and a band played on the nearby stage.

Amid an exhausting discussion with the mayor on the thorny subject of school-age vaccinations, a deep voice suddenly sounded behind her. "Dance with me."

She accepted and bid the mayor good evening. Seth led her to the dance floor.

She let him guide her, even as she protested. "Your leg."

"It's a slow song. I can manage a sway. Just don't ask me to promenade."

"I have no idea how to do that."

"Then we're good." He hooked his cane onto his forearm before placing one hand on hers and his other on her hip.

She glanced around, noticing a few stares directed their way, and then she saw Gregg for the first time that night.

He stood on the edge of the dance floor, watching her

dance with Seth. He looked confused rather than angry. The Sheriff wore jeans and a plaid shirt and had apparently left his signature hat at home. His gun, though, still rested on his hip.

"You look stunning," Seth said, oblivious to Gregg's stare.

She turned back to face her dance partner. "You clean up decently too, you know—when you're not making a bloody mess of my car and kitchen."

Seth chuckled. "I want to see you again, Vanessa."

She wanted to remind him that they lived two *very* different lives—and how would they bridge that distance? But such a statement would betray that her interest in him ran deep enough that she was already considering the ramifications of a long-term relationship. Wouldn't that make her seem just a little crazy? After knowing Seth for all of three days?

You're worried about what the man who claims to see ghosts thinks about your relationship prognostication?

"Oh my." Seth grimaced. He moved closer, putting her arms around his neck and his hands on her waist. "You seem to be processing a lot behind those baby blues."

"There's a lot to process." She felt breathless at their proximity.

"I'm only asking for a date. I'll tie up loose ends with Julio, and then we can go out for drinks—or a movie, or putt-putt. I don't even know what they have around here to do for fun, but you haven't said yes, yet, so I'll keep rambling to avoid awkward silence."

Vanessa chuckled. "Yes, alright. A date."

He made her laugh, and no man had done that—nor

made her feel so at ease in his embrace—for as long as she could remember.

"Whew. I was beginning to worry it'd been so long since I'd last asked a woman out, I'd lost my touch."

She glanced down at his hands around her waist. "You certainly haven't lost *that*." His touch, she meant.

Seth lowered his voice. "I've thought about kissing you from the first moment I saw you."

She stared up at him. The prospect of kissing Seth both thrilled and terrified her. Why was she reading so much into the chemistry between them? She felt too vulnerable to give in to her feelings.

"Be my Valentine, Vanessa."

Something flickered through the sky before coming to rest on Seth's shoulder. Vanessa gasped. It was a vibrant blue butterfly, which gently opened and closed his wings as it perched there.

Oh, Alex.

Vanessa leaned forward and pressed her lips against Seth's. The brief, sweet kiss dissolved all the vulnerability she'd felt and instantly gave way to strength.

When she leaned back, Seth's expression looked as surprised as she felt.

"*Tu ternura me encanta.*" He brushed his hand along her cheek.

"Uh oh. Spanish. Does this mean Rico's back?"

Seth smiled. "No. I said, 'I love your tenderness.'"

The music stopped before a change in song.

"Can I get you something to drink?" he asked.

"I'd like that."

He slid his cane down from where he'd rested it on his forearm. Together, they walked toward the beverage bar.

Gregg appeared before her. "Can I have this dance?"

Startled, she nodded as Gregg took her hand and led her away from Seth.

The Sheriff's cheeks were flushed red, but his smile appeared genuine—if a little sad. She'd never meant to hurt Gregg's feelings.

"Your friend said he was passing through town. When does he leave?"

She glanced back at Seth, whose back was to her as he stood in line. "Tomorrow." Her voice betrayed her disappointment.

"How long have you known him?"

"Not long enough."

"What does he do?"

"Law enforcement. Right now, he's recovering from an injury. I'm not sure what's after that." Would Seth go back to the DEA? Could he even go back with his cover blown? Plus, he needed time to heal.

"You like him?"

The Sheriff and his interrogation. Gregg wasn't being unkind, but he hadn't even bothered to ask Vanessa how her day had been. The entire town buzzed about the life she'd saved today, but Gregg was more worried about a stranger passing through town.

"I like him, Gregg, probably more than I should for a guy just passing through. Crick likes him, too."

"Crick likes everyone."

"Seth laughs at my jokes, and he makes me laugh."

And he cooks me meals.

And Alex approves of him.

Seth stood in the bar line when he was intercepted by the sudden appearance of Rico's shimmering apparition.

"I just spotted Julio. He's *here*."

Seth felt the hairs on the back of his neck rise. He turned and looked through the crowd, searching the perimeter. "You couldn't have given me a little more notice?"

"I'm sorry, *hombre*," Rico said.

Seth spotted Julio quickly, leaning against a tree in the shadows with the plump Val beside him. Julio had been watching him, and he gave Seth a feral grin. Then, he opened his jacket and flashed the holster of his gun at him.

Seth's stomach plummeted. He urgently considered his options. He was unarmed and certainly not in any condition to run and try to lead Julio away from the civilians. His only option was surrender.

Perhaps once Julio led him far enough away from the crowd, Seth could try a counterattack, but his chances of surviving were slim. Julio hadn't scaled as high in the ranks of the organization by being clumsy or stupid.

"Looks like I'll be joining you real soon, Rico."

Seth started walking toward Julio, slow and steady with his cane.

"No. No," Rico protested. "I can do something—maybe a distraction with the lights or shaking the tree leaves."

"No. Do nothing. Anything that attracts the crowd's attention puts everyone here in danger."

When Seth was only a few feet away, Julio smirked. "The elusive DEA agent. You're out of lives, *traidor*. That way." He jutted his chin in the direction of Main Street, leading away from the crowd.

Seth led as Julio followed. The Mexican drug dealer drew his gun but kept it low and close to his body. Seth had no way of easily disarming him.

"After I take care of you, I take care of that *mujer guapa*."

The 'pretty woman' Julio referred to was Vanessa. He'd clearly seen them dancing together.

"She's nothing," Seth insisted, gut twisting. "Just a means to an end. A place to hide."

A low, sinister laugh emitted from Julio. *"Amores, humo y tos, no pueden estar secretos."*

Love, smoke, and cough are hard to hide.

Seth's chest tightened. His feelings for Vanessa were probably obvious. Five years undercover posing convincingly as another criminal in the heart of Julio's organization, and now he'd followed up that performance by completely failing to keep his feelings for Vanessa concealed.

Now, his enemy knew his weakness.

Seth would have to bide his time and wait for an opening to make his move. He couldn't sacrifice his life to prevent the crowd in the gardens from harm, only to have Julio then go after Vanessa to enact his revenge.

95

Vanessa danced with Gregg, but kept the distance between them platonic. The electric blue butterfly reappeared, this time fluttering above the crowd of dancers. Vanessa's eyes followed the flapping of its wings as it made its way above the beverage bar.

Seth wasn't there.

Vanessa snapped her head from side to side to scan the gardens, but she didn't see him.

Alex, what are you trying to tell me?

Two more butterflies joined the first.

"That's odd," Gregg said, noting the butterflies.

"I have to go."

"Vanessa, wait."

She left Gregg and followed the butterflies. They looked like tiny sparks of electricity, floating through the air as they led her away from the gardens and the pink, glowing lights of the dance.

She walked down a darkened Main Street, passing the emporium, the bakery, and then the café and boutiques. Everything had closed down for tonight's festivities.

Her low heels clicked on the concrete as the sound of the band and the boisterous chatter faded behind her.

The butterflies, now an enlarging conglomerate of a dozen or so, turned down an alleyway. Her heart hammered in her chest as she turned to peer into the alley, darkened by its long looming shadows. As fear snaked along her spine, she remembered that the gun Seth had insisted she take tonight was still in the glove compartment of her car.

Then, she saw him.

"Seth!"

He knelt on the ground, facing a dark-skinned man in black clothing who was pointing a gun at Seth's head. Beside Seth lurked a potbellied Mexican, watching the execution about to be... well, *executed*.

But then the gunman heard her cry and jerked the barrel in Vanessa's direction instead.

"No!" Seth sprang forward, launching his shoulder into his would-be executioner's midsection with the full weight of his muscular body behind it.

A wild shot sent a bullet into the side of the building behind Vanessa. As Seth wrestled the gunman to the ground, the second Mexican reached for his weapon.

Vanessa was already sprinting towards them to help Seth, but she knew she wouldn't make it in time. The thug stood far enough away that he could draw his weapon and shoot either Seth *or* her long before she could reach him— not that she even had a plan for when she did. Each gunman was at least twice her size.

As the second gunman raised his weapon, the butter- flies drifting above him abruptly descended, plunging down like dive-bombers. The gunman shrieked, swatting the fluttering insects as they blinded him.

Vanessa never slowed. She snatched up Seth's cane from the ground and swung it like a baseball bat directly into the man's knee. He screamed and fell to the ground.

She brought her second blow down across the man's forearms, causing him to drop the gun with another outburst of pain.

To her right, Seth landed a bone-crunching blow to the face of the man he was wrestling with before snatching the gun from him.

"Sheriff's Department! Nobody move!"

A loud voice rang down the alleyway. Vanessa turned to see Gregg striding toward them, gun raised. "Drop your weapons!"

Seth set the gun down, raising his hands. Vanessa dropped the cane. Panting for air, she leaned against one wall. The other two men lay on the concrete of the alleyway, staring up at the Sheriff.

She looked at Seth, whose color had drained to a pale caramel. Blood soaked through his jeans where his bullet wound had clearly reopened. She moved slowly toward him, throwing a glance to the Sheriff as he covered them all with his service pistol.

"It's okay, Gregg. He's DEA." She pointed to the red stain soaking Seth's jeans. "Let me look at his bullet wound."

"Let me clear the scene of these weapons first." Gregg picked up the two guns that lay discarded on the ground, never once lowering his own.

With the weapons secured, he nodded at Vanessa. "Go ahead."

He kept his weapon trained on Seth's attacker, who lay crumpled on the floor.

Vanessa helped ease Seth into a sitting position with his back against the wall. Behind them, Gregg called his deputy for assistance.

Vanessa worked frantically. The lights of the alleyway, consisting of all the low-watt bulbs installed above the rear doors of the town stores, were too dim for a proper physical exam. She tore off one of Seth's shirtsleeves and used it to secure the existing bandages over his wounds.

He laughed weakly. "I like you ripping my clothes off."

Hands shaking from the adrenaline, she cinched the cloth tighter. He grimaced.

"I told you I needed your protection," Seth winced. "Still, you shouldn't have run into danger like that."

"Why did you wander off?" Vanessa demanded.

"I didn't wander off! Julio led me at gunpoint away from the crowd. He was going to execute me right here."

"Why didn't you shout for help?"

"So he could shoot into the crowd and kill civilians?"

Vanessa sighed, unable to argue with his logic.

"How'd you find me?"

A lone azure butterfly gently landed on Vanessa's shoulder, seemingly from nowhere. She glanced at it as her eyes grew moist. "Alex."

Seth cupped her chin and pulled Vanessa close, touching their foreheads together.

"You scared the hell out of me, Vanessa. Promise me you'll *never* pull another stunt like that again."

"Well, if *you* promise not to get taken down another dark alleyway at gunpoint again, I won't have to."

SETH LEANED back against the wall of the alleyway and closed his eyes. His leg pulsed with pain. After Vanessa had stopped the bleeding, she'd stepped away to explain events to Gregg.

"She saved your life, *hombre*," Rico said.

"Yeah, for a second time."

"She wouldn't risk her life for just anyone."

"Oh, I get that she likes me, but I also get that she's leery of making an emotional investment when our career paths might take us in separate directions. She's already been through that with that surgeon."

"*Tarda una hora en conocerte y solo un dia en enamorarme. Pero me llevará toda una vida poder olvidarte,*" Rico said.

Seth had heard the saying before, and it rang true for his situation, *It took me an hour to know you and only a day to fall in love—but it will take me a lifetime to be able to forget you.*

Rico shrugged. "Your alias is blown for any more undercover work, anyway. You're going to spend the next year in depositions dismantling Julio's operation. There's an office in Laredo. You can commute."

Seth's heart lifted a little. "Yes, I can."

When Gregg came over to him, Seth struggled to stand. Vanessa lingered at the far end of the alleyway, watching and waiting.

"How's the leg?" the Sheriff asked. He held a notepad in his hand and the Sheriff's signature campaign hat was back on his head.

"No worse for wear."

"Vanessa tells me your name is Seth Dellosa, and you're undercover DEA."

Seth looked around the alleyway. Halfway down the alley, closer to Vanessa, Gregg's deputy already had Val secured and was cuffing Julio while reading him his rights.

"I was, but I'm not so much undercover anymore."

"I'm going to need to question you about the events of tonight, and I'll need your boss' contact information. The only reason I'm not arresting you right now is because Vanessa vouches for you."

An ambulance was parked at the end of the alleyway near Vanessa, bathing the narrow passageway in red and white lights.

Seth shifted his weight. "That's my ride. You can find me in the ER."

"I won't have to find you. Deputy Taylor will be going with you."

Seth shrugged.

Abruptly, a commotion caught his eye.

Deputy Taylor had been bent over, about to secure the handcuffs, when Julio suddenly struggled free. With one cuff dangling from his wrist, Julio desperately yanked the deputy's sidearm from his belt, swinging it around to take aim at Vanessa.

Gregg shouted in alarm, snatching for his sidearm, but Seth was faster.

He wrenched Gregg's SIG Sauer semiautomatic from the Sheriff's belt and aimed instinctively, staring down the gunsight at Julio.

Seth squeezed the trigger. There was a flash, a deafening roar that echoed off the walls of the alleyway, and then a choking cloud of smoke.

At the other end of the alleyway, Julio fell to the ground. The deputy's stolen gun clattered to the concrete, unfired.

VANESSA ARRIVED home to find it dark and lonely. Crick greeted her, but even he seemed subdued.

Seth was gone.

After Seth had shot Julio, Gregg had one of his deputies take her off site, grumbling something about scene safety. Vanessa had protested—after all, it wasn't as if she'd never seen dead bodies in her career.

Gregg had insisted on stuffing her in the backseat of a patrol car, regardless. Through the glass, she'd watched as Seth was loaded into the ambulance on a stretcher. Then, after she'd finished being questioned by Gregg—whose demeanor suggested he'd gone from viewing her as the sweet young woman he wanted to court, to a bizarre thrill-seeker with secrets—she'd gone to the emergency room to find Seth.

He wasn't there.

The ER doctor said he'd cleaned Seth's reopened wound, after which some official-looking men had swept Seth away.

So, that was it, then. The ball now rested in Seth's court. He could follow-up on his claim to want to see Vanessa again, or he might never come back.

He'd now saved *her* life. That made them even, if anybody was keeping score. Vanessa wasn't. She just wanted Seth back in her life, especially now that the danger had abated.

On her porch, in the darkness, she patted Crick before heading inside and toward her bedroom. She stepped straight into the shower.

Then, exhausted but clean, she finally crawled into bed and closed her eyes.

CHAPTER 10

Seth wrapped up a grueling week of meetings and debriefings. He'd detailed the entire *Las Arañas* organization to the DEA. Julio was dead, and Val was in county lockup.

Jody Green walked with him out of the conference room.

"So—vacation?" Jody took off his spectacles and cleaned them with a cloth from his front shirt pocket.

"I've got five years of accumulated unused vacation," Seth said. "I guess I can use those months to figure out my next career move."

"With your skills, you could go anywhere in South America."

"Not undercover again. I'm done with undercover."

Jody nodded and scratched his balding head, as if he'd anticipated that answer.

"I'm going to take some time off," Seth mused.

"You know, if you're done with undercover work, we

could certainly use your experience in teaching the younger agents."

Seth looked down at the cane in his hand. "Now you're making me sound like an old man."

"*Experienced,*" Jody corrected. "Seasoned."

"Where would I be stationed?"

"With your skills? Not to mention the reputation you've earned by dismantling Julio Oquiñena and his spider cartel? I'd say you have your pick of spots anywhere in Texas."

Seth recalled the DEA station in Laredo, but the San Antonio office would be a faster drive down I-37. "I'll think about it, and I'll be in touch."

He shook hands with Jody and parted ways.

Deep thoughts about Seth's future swirled around his mind as he left the office and got into his car. A life without lies, in the company of the woman he'd fallen in love with, sounded like the most tempting future he could have envisioned.

To that end, the Laredo station was closer to Vanessa.

"Are you going back to the doctor lady?" Rico asked.

Seth squeezed the rubber dog bone he'd bought for Crick in one hand as he drove down the highway. "You think she wants me? And all of my baggage?"

"Only one way to find out."

"What about you, my friend? What can I do to help you find peace and move on?" Seth liked Rico's company, but only spirits with unfinished business lingered on Earth. Seth wanted his friend and partner to have peace.

"When you're not *Las Arañas'* enemy number one, and

things cool off in Mexico, you can find my mother and you can tell her I love her."

"I'll do you one better," Seth promised. "I'll tell her you saved my life and brought a drug cartel to its knees as you did so. We couldn't have taken down Julio without you ... or your sacrifice."

"Yeah, that sounds pretty good," Rico said wistfully. "*Bueno, ya me voy*, Dellosa."

"*Cuídese. Adiós*, Valez."

Rico's apparition in the passenger seat grew more and more translucent until he finally vanished altogether.

VANESSA FINISHED her drills at the batting cage and pulled off her helmet. By her estimation, she'd hit ten home runs, a dozen triples, thirty-six doubles, and fifty singles against the pitching machine.

She left the batting cage, climbing into her Ford Fiesta to drive home. A week had passed since the Valentine's dance, and Vanessa had put in long work hours to make up for the prior week.

On Monday, she'd received a text message from an unknown number.

I'm tied up with work. I'll call you as soon as I can and set up that date.
—Jorge

She'd struggled with how to reply. A simple 'OK' couldn't convey her delight in hearing from Seth or the agonizing anticipation of waiting to see him. Vanessa couldn't think of a humorous response that couldn't be misconstrued in a text message, but she also didn't want to send an emoji that might portray her as incapable of expressing herself through words.

After much debate, she'd finally settled on, *I look forward to seeing you.*

To which Seth had responded: *:)*

Laughing, Vanessa had pocketed her phone and went back to work, not knowing if Seth would be tied up for a week, or a month, or longer.

Her phone buzzed.

She took the call on her car's Bluetooth speakerphone.

"Hello?"

"Hey, it's Kailee. I know it's not a workday, but I ran into the Coramonds at the grocery store. Maxwell was discharged from the hospital a few days ago, and they want to make a follow-up appointment with you. I put him down for Thursday."

"Great. On Monday, can you have the hospital fax us his discharge summary so I can review that on his clinic day?"

"Will do."

"Thanks."

As Vanessa pulled into her driveway, arms aching after the hours spent in the batting cages, she saw Seth sitting on her porch petting Crick.

He wore cowboy boots, jeans, and a crisp, baby-blue button-down shirt.

Vanessa's breath caught.

"I... I have to go," she told Kailee, fumbling for the icon to disconnect the call.

"Everything okay?"

Vanessa stared at Seth as she put the car in park. "Yes, I'm home..."

She paused.

"...and maybe so is the love of my life."

"Huh?"

"I'll explain later." Vanessa turned off the engine and got out of the car.

As she straightened, Seth stood and limped down the steps. He had a smile of uncertainty, as if she might not receive him well—as if he was worried he might have only imagined their brief three days together had changed her life the way it had changed his.

She decided to squash that uncertainty by dashing into his arms and wrapping her arms around his neck. "You came back!"

"Of course I did. I'm your Valentine."

Crick gave a single woof at a blue butterfly suddenly fluttering around the porch.

Vanessa grinned, hugging Seth tightly as she looked up and spoke to the butterfly.

"Yes, thanks, Alex—I get that you like Seth."

When the butterflies had saved her life in the alleyway, Vanessa had given even more credence to Seth's claim of being able to speak to ghosts.

With one arm on her hip, he tucked strands of red hair behind one of her ears. His eyes sparkled with adoration.

"What about Rico?" Vanessa asked.

"He has closure, so he's moved on."

She glanced at the butterfly now resting on the porch railing.

"I suspect that Alex will always keep an eye out for you," Seth said.

"And you?" Vanessa asked.

"Oh, I'll be keeping *both* eyes on you."

Seth hoisted her up, and she wrapped her legs around his waist. He barely winced, despite the injury in his leg.

When their lips collided, she felt his warmth rush through her like a seventy-mile-per-hour, fast-pitch softball.

Finally, they pulled away from the kiss.

She stared into his bright emerald eyes. "Oh, no. Your leg."

She started to squirm down, but he held her tightly against him, supporting her weight with his arms under her thighs.

"Oh! No, you don't. I'm not ready to let go yet."

Vanessa ran a hand through Seth's hair and down his clean-shaven, smooth jawline. "When *are* you going to let me go?"

"Maybe never, Vanessa. Maybe never."

She smiled and kissed him again.

READY FOR ANOTHER sweet and magical romantic suspense? There are so many delights to enjoy! Keep reading for an excerpt from the next book.

. . .

INDIVIDUAL BOOKS

Romancing the Spirit Series #1
Sadie's Spirit / Willow's Windfall
Cassie's Chase / Phoebe's Pharaoh
Vanessa's Valentine / Autumn's Angel
Romancing the Spirit Series #2
Carol's Christmas / Allison's Alibi
Gracelynn's Genie / Michelle's Miracle
Heather's Hero / Chloe's Cupid
Romancing the Spirit Series #3
Sabrina's Storm / Jenny's Justice
Stella's Star / Gigi's Gift
Phoenix's Phantom / Fiona's Freedom

THE CHRISTMAS COLLECTION

DEAR READER

Want to keep in touch?

If you enjoyed this book and want to know about future releases by CB Samet, you can CLICK HERE to sign up for my mailing list! I promise I won't spam you. I only send an email when I have a new book released, giveaways, or special discounts. You can also unsubscribe at any time.

If you loved this book, kindly let others know by posing a brief comment on social media or leave a review where you purchased it so readers can find their next favorite romantic suspense series.

Even more ways to follow me below!

Thank you for reading,

CB Samet

OTHER BOOKS BY CB SAMET

Looking for more romantic suspense? How about with an urban fantasy twist? More heat, more action.

Check out The Shadow Guardians trilogy.

Get *Raven's Flight, a prequel novella* for FREE. In my newsletter, you'll learn about me, special discounts, and new releases.

Raven's Flight, prequel novella

Raine Down, Book 1

Rosalyn's Run, novella

Storm Surge, Book 2

Anka's Orb, novella

Sky Fall, Book 3

～

Meridian File / Masters File / Box Set 1

McMillan File / Maltisse File / Box Set 2

Storm File / Sullivan File / Box Set 3

Sharp File / Sizani File / Box Set 4

Rivera File / Rucker File / Box Set 5

Richmond File / Redwood File / Box Set 6

Atlas File / Angel File / Box Set 7

～

Olympian Awakenings Trilogy

Urban fantasy Greek Mythology Adventure

Grab the prequel exclusively HERE.

Stone Hearts

Winds of Destiny

Flame and Shadow

∾

The Dr. Whyte Adventure Novels
Thriller Series

Black Gold

Whyte Knight

Gray Horizon

∾

Love action/adventure and strong female leads in a fantasy world? Check out my other genre:

The Avant Champion Fantasy Series

The Avant Champion: Rising

Malakai: An Avant Champion Origin of Malos Story (prequel)

The Avant Champion: Honor

The Avant Champion: Ashes

Brothers' Bond: An Avant Champion Malakai Story

The Avant Champion: Conquest

Isabel: An Avant Champion novelette

The Avant Champion: Redeem

AUTUMN'S ANGEL

An eyewitness torn from hiding. An FBI agent with an agenda. And all hell breaks loose on Halloween night.

Devlin Angelo is attempting to live an inconspicuous life in witness protection—easier said than done when one talks to ghosts. But a murder in his office throws unwanted attraction in his direction, and Devlin's secrets are no longer safe. With the help of a ghost, he hopes to escape those hunting him.

FBI Agent Autumn Bently is hot on the trail of fraudulent art. When her prime suspect is shot, mysterious psychic reader, Devlin Angelo, is her only link to finding the art and solving her case. But murder raises the stakes and nothing is as it seems when Autumn comes in contact with the paranormal. Yet embracing the paranormal might be her only way to save Devlin.

SAMPLE CHAPTER

Autumn Bentley's mark glanced over his shoulder before walking into a small building with a flashing neon sign:

```
DEVLIN'S PSYCHIC READINGS
```

Under the near-midday sun, the short, stocky Bernard Warden vanished from Autumn's view. Why would a smuggler go to a fortune-teller? Unless this place was a front for hiding stolen or fake goods.

The single story, brick rectangular structure had a gable roof. Outside the front door, carved pumpkins displayed their crooked smiles.

She needed to get her eyes and ears on the inside of that building, but she wouldn't learn anything by barging through the front door. Walking around back, she glanced around at the other commercial shops and tried to look inconspicuous in broad daylight.

Finding the back entrance, obscured by five-foot-tall summersweet bushes on either side, she tested the doorknob. Locked.

Bending down, she noticed the plants' late-summer blooms had withered and fallen to the ground as their leaves transformed to a vibrant yellow for the fall. Withdrawing her lock pick, she set to work on the simple latch bolt on a rotating knob.

When the lock gave way, she eased herself inside a kitchenette. It had a small refrigerator, microwave, and a round, two-seater table. Following the sound of voices, Autumn crept down a hallway. Hanging purple beads glinted over an archway that led to a front room. She hugged one wall and squinted through the beads.

Bernard, Autumn's mark, sat at a round table decorated with a shimmering purple tablecloth, on top of which perched a clear orb. Across the table from Bernard sat a gray-bearded man in a cheap black tuxedo. He wore an oversized black top hat as he hunched over, staring at tarot cards spread on the table. Was this man Devlin, the owner of DEVLIN'S PSYCHIC READINGS, or was Devlin a *nom de plume*?

The room had dark paneled walls, and thick purple drapes filtered sunlight down to a faint glow. Candles and incense smelling of cinnamon burned on a decorative stand against one wall.

Autumn frowned. She thought she would catch Bernard elbow deep in illicit activity, not doing a tarot card reading. There had to be more transpiring here than met the eye. Perhaps this silver-bearded charlatan ran a front for forged art.

She rolled her shoulders, feeling the weight of her Glock in its harness. She would discover the secret of this clandestine meeting, even if it meant eavesdropping throughout the entire preposterous psychic reading.

Devlin shuffled the deck of tarot cards. His customer seated on the opposite side of the round table was a regular. Bernard visited Devlin once a month to commune with Joy, his deceased ex-wife. He'd initially come to see his grandmother, but Devlin could only see ghosts who hadn't crossed over yet. Spirits at rest couldn't be summoned. When Devlin tried for Bernard's grandmother, he'd received no reply.

Of Bernard's relatives, his ex-wife was the only one still lingering. So he came to speak with Joy monthly and have Devlin read his future. Devlin had explained that tarot cards weren't his strong suit and couldn't reliably predict the future, but Bernard came faithfully, paid faithfully, and listened with rapt attention. The interaction seemed to be helping both him and his ex-wife as they mended their relationship from across the grave, and Joy encouraged Bernard to become a better man.

Joy, a boisterous Southern belle in her fifties, had a great beehive of bleach blonde hair and an even bigger heart. She talked incessantly in a sticky-sweet Southern drawl, but Bernard only heard what Devlin filtered down to him.

As Devlin read the tarot cards, Joy floated nearby and observed her ex-husband's reaction. Devlin flipped the third card face up on the table—Death. He cleared his throat and scooped up the cards to reshuffle.

"What was that?"

"Nothing, sir. Let's do it again." Devlin masked his normal voice with a fake British accent. He was probably butchering the accent, but no one who came for psychic readings to a shack in Sacramento would be able to tell the difference.

After shuffling, Devlin turned over the top card— Death again.

"Death?" Bernard asked in a croak.

"Sometimes death is a new beginning." Devlin could hear his own voice losing the elderly tone and accented disguise as the hair on the back of his neck stood on end. He'd never had the Death card rear its ugly head.

The card didn't necessarily represent physical death. It often meant a change, such as a relationship or a career change. Yet, Devlin sensed doom as he touched a finger to the skeleton figure on the card.

Joy crossed her translucent arms. "Well, Lordy! Ain't that a hot mess. I reckon Bernard's gettin' the short end of the stick. He'll be joining me soon."

Devlin looked up at the bulbous spirit of Bernard's ex-wife. Joy had died of a heart attack a year ago, but she and Bernard had already been divorced for about five years. She'd divorced him when he'd refused to quit his illegal activities, after which she remarried and became Joy Porter.

"What's it mean?" Bernard asked. His expression of wide-eyed worry and his jutting jaw had him looking like a spooked filly.

Joy's transparent face looked solemn. "Honey, that's as ominous as dark clouds before a hurricane. Somethin' gawd-awful is about to put his knickers in a knot."

The front door burst open. A tall thin figure, who might have been a skeleton of Death himself, stood haloed in light from the midday sun. The man raised a gun and fired.

Autumn heard the splintering of wood as someone kicked in the front door. A lanky man fired two successive shots aimed at Bernard.

Bernard fell back in his chair, landing on the floor

with a thud. Simultaneously, the fortune-teller dove behind the table, his hat flying off his head.

As Autumn pulled her Glock, she shouted, "FBI! Freeze!"

The gunman wasted no time in firing his weapon at Autumn. She quickly crouched back behind the wall, but as the bullets punctured the thin plaster walls, Autumn realized she didn't have much cover. She counted the number of bullets fired as splinters flew around her. She'd glimpsed the assailant's Ruger SR22. At most, he had ten bullets before he'd have to reload.

After the tenth round, she leapt up and pressed through the beads hanging in the archway, prepared to return fire. But the figure had vanished.

Heart pounding, Autumn surveyed the scene as she cautiously passed through the room with gun raised. Bernard lay sprawled on the floor with the other man—presumably the psychic reader, Devlin—kneeling over him. Autumn couldn't be sure if Devlin had been injured as well.

"Stay down!" she barked.

When Autumn reached the doorway, she cautiously scanned the perimeter. The sound of a car engine caught her attention. She sprinted after it. As she slowed and took aim at the front tire, the driver-side window lowered.

"Crap!" She dove to the side and rolled onto the lawn as the gunman fired again. Behind her, one of the pumpkins erupted. By the time Autumn tumbled and sprang to her feet, the car had swerved onto the main road and accelerated away from her.

Holstering her gun, Autumn swore. She shook out an ache in her left arm. She must have jarred something when she rolled. She walked back into Devlin's lair and pulled out her phone.

"9-1-1. What's your emergency?"

"Gunshot victim." Autumn gave the address as she looked down at Bernard, lying in a pool of his own blood.

Devlin, who was surprisingly not shrieking in terror at the shootout and man bleeding on his purple carpet, was administering first aid. He'd stripped his table of the purple cloth and applied pressure to Bernard's chest wound.

With EMS activated, Autumn disconnected the call and took a steadying breath. The police would arrive soon, and she didn't have time for local PD stalling her case. But she couldn't leave the scene of a crime. At the very least, she needed to get information from this charlatan before the police took him out of her reach.

"What did Bernard say to you before he was shot?"

"What?" Devlin sounded breathless from his effort.

"You were talking to Bernard before the hitman arrived. What were you talking about?"

"How to make cherry pie," he snapped.

"What?"

He glared up at her. "I'm a medium. What do you think we were talking about?"

Autumn narrowed her eyes and knelt down beside him, careful not to interfere with his first-aid efforts. Devlin's voice sounded all wrong. His wasn't the voice of an old British aristocrat—not as it had been earlier. He sounded young and American. With his hat off, disheveled dark-brown hair was visible. She scrutinized the silver strands of hair jutting off the man's chin—coarse, synthetic hair. If Autumn had one gift, it was how to spot a fake.

She tugged off the fake beard, revealing a handsome face and green eyes on a man who looked to be about thirty-five.

"Do you mind?" he snapped. A young Devlin rocked back on his heels and wiped the blood from his hands onto the tablecloth.

"Are you injured?" she asked him.

He stared at Bernard, who gazed lifelessly at the ceiling.

Autumn snapped her fingers close to Devlin's face. "Hey! Cherry Pie! Are you injured?"

"No. But Bernard is dead."

"Should we do CPR?"

Devlin turned his blazing green eyes in her direction. "Cardiopulmonary resuscitation requires a functioning cardiopulmonary circuit. He no longer has one. He doesn't have any blood left to circulate. He's dead." Devlin turned away from her and appeared to be speaking to Bernard. "I'm sorry."

"I need to know your relationship with this man and everything he's told you."

The magician blinked at her. "Why?"

"He's part of an FBI investigation."

"Can I see some ID?"

Autumn obliged, showing him her credentials as Agent Bentley of the FBI from her wallet before tucking it back in her jacket pocket.

The man nodded and looked up at her. The hat had disheveled his hair. He turned his sad gaze back to Bernard briefly before looking at Autumn again, this time with panicked worry in his expression.

"You called 9-1-1."

Autumn arched an eyebrow. "Most people do when someone's been shot."

Devlin stood and placed a finger to his temple. "I can't be here when the police get here."

His alarm surprised her, but he seemed afraid and not dangerous.

"Are you wanted for something?" she asked.

The accusatory tone of her voice had his eyes narrowing, and he took a step back. She held his gaze, waiting for an answer.

Devlin turned, hastening toward the kitchenette. "I have to go." He shrugged out of his penguin jacket.

"You're not leaving the crime scene. And I need to see some identification."

Who was this man pretending to be an old psychic, and why was he so fearful of the police? Autumn exposed frauds constantly in her job, and she would expose this one, too, good looks aside.

<<<BUY AUTUMN'S ANGEL TODAY>>>